Noah came toward her, his gaze growing softer....

"I'll call Aunt Arletta to let her know I'll be home later," Ivy murmured to fill the quiet. She rested against the doorway, her hands folded across her waist.

"All right." Noah stood very close. His breath fanned her cheek. His proximity unnerved her. It simply wasn't fair to have this reaction when he was so...so unsuitable for her ten-year plan.

"Shall we take my truck, or your car?" he asked with a mischievous grin. He placed his palm high against the door frame just above her head. The light in his eyes made her breath catch in her throat, and all she could think of was that kiss they'd shared in the kitchen. How sweet his lips had felt on hers...

How afterward she'd vowed to never let him kiss her again.

She wouldn't let her heart get involved, Ivy told herself for the dozenth time.

She wouldn't allow herself to fall in love with Noah Thornton!

Books by Ruth Scofield

Love Inspired

In God's Own Time #29
The Perfect Groom #65

RUTH SCOFIELD

became serious about writing after she'd raised her children. Until then, she'd concentrated her life on being a June Cleaver-type wife and mother, spent years as a Bible student and teacher for teens and young adults, and led a weekly women's prayer group. When she'd made a final wedding dress and her last child had left the nest, she declared to one and all that it was her turn to activate a dream. Thankfully her husband applauded her decision.

Ruth began school in an old-fashioned rural two-room schoolhouse and grew up in the days before television, giving substance to her notion that she still has one foot in the last century. However, active involvement with six rambunctious grandchildren has her eagerly looking forward to the next millennium. After living on the East Coast for years, Ruth and her husband now live in Missouri.

The Perfect Groom

Ruth Scofield

Published by Steeple Hill Books™

If you purchased this book without a cover you should be aware that this book is stolen property. It was reported as "unsold and destroyed" to the publisher, and neither the author nor the publisher has received any payment for this "stripped book."

STEEPLE HILL BOOKS

ISBN 0-373-87065-5

THE PERFECT GROOM

Copyright © 1999 by Ruth Scofield Schmidt

All rights reserved. Except for use in any review, the reproduction or utilization of this work in whole or in part in any form by any electronic, mechanical or other means, now known or hereafter invented, including xerography, photocopying and recording, or in any information storage or retrieval system, is forbidden without the written permission of the editorial office, Steeple Hill Books, 300 East 42nd Street, New York, NY 10017 U.S.A.

All characters in this book have no existence outside the imagination of the author and have no relation whatsoever to anyone bearing the same name or names. They are not even distantly inspired by any individual known or unknown to the author, and all incidents are pure invention.

This edition published by arrangement with Steeple Hill Books.

® and TM are trademarks of Steeple Hill Books, used under license. Trademarks indicated with ® are registered in the United States Patent and Trademark Office, the Canadian Trade Marks Office and in other countries.

Look us up on-line at: http://www.steeplehill.com

Printed in U.S.A.

This is for all the many affectionate, loving aunts who enrich our lives with their presence, their advice and guidance, their constancy and support. Most of mine have gone from this earth, but I recall them to memory with great fondness and longing to see them again.

And for the aunt for whom I was named, who is lively and shining with love—Aunt Ruth. Everyone should be so blessed.

By wisdom a house is built, and through understanding it is established; through knowledge its rooms are filled with rare and beautiful treasures.

—*Proverbs* 24:3-4

Chapter One

Ivy hated weddings. She despised bridesmaids dresses. She still abhorred all ten attendant gowns already stuffed in the back of her closet, used once, never appropriate for any other occasion. Never mind the two once-in-a-dream white bridal gowns, unused, forlorn, and stored in plastic covers, hidden away in disappointment and disgust.

She especially detested the bright lime-green silk that clung too tightly to her generous curves at this very moment, but she'd bitten her tongue over the choice. After all, she'd given her word to support the bride, her best friend Kelly, and Kelly's sister wanted this style, this color.

"Ivy Suzanne York, quit pulling at your dress," Aunt Arletta said, scarcely lowering her voice as she steered her from behind the huge oak where Ivy had tried to hide. "You're not a child, you know."

Ivy swallowed a snappy response, eyeing the man her aunt had tugged along a few minutes ago in her wake.

No, Ivy hadn't been a child for a long time. At twenty-seven, college educated, with ten solid years of retail experience behind her, and now owner of her own shop, Ivy considered herself well and truly grown. A responsible person. With nothing to prove to anyone. With a reasonable five-year plan for her life. Never mind that she was more than two years behind her schedule to be married by age twenty-five. But Aunt Arletta, dear as she was, sometimes still treated her as if she couldn't wipe her own nose.

"Ivy, this is Noah Thornton. He has a true artistic eye, don't you think?" The older woman swept her hand wide, indicating the vast grounds surrounding Reeves House, the lovely old stone mansion the bride's parents had rented for the wedding. Ivy hoped to explore more of the grounds later during the reception. Right now, she resented having her few minutes of respite from all the gushy wedding talk stolen by another of her aunt's antics.

It didn't help her mood any when the dark-eyed man standing two feet in front of her smirked as he nodded a greeting. Glints of amusement sparked from his warm brown eyes as his gaze swept down her figure before returning to her face.

"Noah, this is my niece, Ivy. She has the shop I told you about, 'Wall's Intrigue' in Brookside. Seems to me you two have a lot in common. You in landscaping and she in interior design." Aunt Arletta, dressed in a burnt orange fall suit that complemented her snowy hair, grasped Ivy's wrist again just as she tried to ease backward. "Noah's unmarried, Ivy, and I'm sure he's looking for just the right young woman to fill his life. Proverbs says, 'A man who finds a wife—' "

"Aunt Arletta!"

Noah's lips twitched into a full grin, his teeth flashing white against his tanned skin, as though he knew Ivy wanted to melt into the shrubbery.

She took in his soiled jeans, damp at the knees, and his heavy work boots. A streak of dirt clung to his forehead, evidence of a swiping arm, no doubt. Behind him, a wheelbarrow full of last-minute bush trimmings sat on the edge of the brick garden terrace. They were less than an hour from the appointed ceremony time; why was a gardener even still on the grounds?

He held a big clay pot of golden mums, the multipetaled blossoms splashing bright color against his denim work shirt. His long fingers showed scabbed knuckles, and Ivy briefly wondered what he'd done to injure his hand.

"But Ivy," Aunt Arletta continued, irrepressible, "Proverbs says, 'A man who finds a wife—'"

"Yes, I know what Proverbs says," Ivy interrupted. She felt her cheeks grow warm with color and pressed her lips together, holding her irritation in check at Aunt Arletta's usual behavior. Introducing her to strange men who her aunt thought suitable husband material was something Ivy'd come to expect. But really! A gardener?

Aunt Arletta knew very well she had her sights set higher. She wanted to meet an upwardly mobile man. Someone who wore expensive suits and silk ties to work and knew the corporate world—or someone solidly entrenched in a good law firm or in line for a hospital chief-of-staff position. A man with a good future.

Pointedly glancing at her watch, she said, "I don't

mean to be rude, Mr., um, Noah, but I've got to get back to the bride. I just ducked out to have a breath of air.''

She glanced around at the banks of autumn flowers and foliage enhancing the walks and benches and terrace. The garden reflected a great deal of work and artistic eye for color and design. ''It all looks lovely, but, er, shouldn't you be finished by now?''

''Just going.'' His voice sounded like deep chocolate icing on a velvet cake. Rich and delicious, it startled her into glancing at him again. She felt her mouth droop in blinking anticipation when he said, ''I'll be out of here in two minutes. Nice to meet you, Ivy.''

He shifted his smile to her aunt, softening his goodbye to her, and ignored Ivy. Nodding almost curtly, she swung on her heel and headed back to the upstairs bedroom set aside as the bride's dressing room.

''I suppose you'll have to find another time to talk to Ivy, Noah,'' she heard her aunt say as she walked away. Then, half-apologetically, ''Weddings make her a bit touchy. And you know, Proverbs says a prudent man overlooks an insult.''

''And only a fool shows his annoyance at once,'' he replied.

Ivy gritted her teeth. Another Proverb, her aunt's favorite source of quotations. Why Aunt Arletta thought she needed to impart that information about her hating weddings flummoxed her. It wasn't a stranger's business to know. It was bad enough for Kelly to watch her like a mother hen whose troublesome chick might run amok, much less having complete strangers expecting her to do something inappropriate. She had every intention of behaving perfectly today. She'd given Kelly her promise.

Still, she paused at the door to take three deep breaths before returning to the bridal party—Kelly, her sister Kathy, and the three other twittering bridesmaids, all wearing identical dresses to her own. She felt like a scoop of lime sherbet. Why couldn't Kathy have gone for the hunter green, like most other autumn weddings sported?

She hoped by this time all the talk between them of whose turn it was next to become a bride had passed. Ivy sighed, allowing herself one moment of defeat before putting on her most dazzling smile. It seemed she would be the last of her high school chums to walk down the isle when she'd been the one who talked most, all her life, of getting married. Thank goodness, Kelly was the only one of the wedding party who knew she'd almost made it to the church twice. Three times, if anyone counted that stupid secret high school engagement, thankfully aborted before the planned elopement took place. She couldn't bear having everyone stare at her in pity, with the unspoken words *three strikes and you're out* hovering in their minds.

Ivy hadn't been lucky at actually becoming a bride.

Now she didn't allow her hopes to jump at every man who might be a likely candidate, and kept her past disappointments locked away in the privacy of her memory bank. But in her heart of hearts she still wished for a husband and a home of her own.

Sudden laughter bubbled up from Ivy's middle; it was a good thing she kept that particular yearning well hidden these days. With Aunt Arletta's propensity for latching onto strange men, she daren't open her mouth. A gardener, for Pete's sake?

Besides, lately she'd decided her life was full enough with the shop, Aunt Arletta and church activities. She helped out in the toddler nursery from time to time, which gave her babies to hug, a momentary feeling of motherhood. A stopgap, to be sure—but who had time for anything else, anyway?

Feeling more serene, Ivy swung through the door and immediately stopped to catch her breath. Fitted with floor-to-ceiling, wall-to-wall mirrors on four sides, the room reflected Kelly's tall, regal figure again and again all around her, stunning in an elegant gown of white lace and satin, trimmed in seed pearls.

"Oh, Kelly," she murmured in awe, instantly scrapping any lingering envy or misplaced jealousy she'd brought into the day. How could she be so petty in light of her friend's happiness? "You'd make the perfect bride to grace any of the brides' magazine covers."

"Thank you, Ivy." Kelly smiled, tremulous with emotion.

Through a connecting door into the next room, the other girls flitted about with lively chatter as they made last-minute checks to their hair and dresses. Strains of a single flute drifted up from the distant first-floor ballroom where the ceremony would take place, shortly joined by violins and a piano.

"Oh, the music has started," Kelly said, her hand fluttering to her chest, a trait unusual for her. "Is it time?"

"Yes," Ivy answered with calm fondness. "Yes it is, hon. And I can't wait 'til Scott gets his first glimpse of you."

Almost two hours later, Ivy finally slipped away from the wedding reception lineup. Her mouth was dryer than a cotton ball and the happy bride no longer needed her. She looked around for the punch table. It stood ten people deep and a multitude of guests stacked the buffet lines; Aunt Arletta moved in one of the lines, busily talking with another woman her own age.

Another half hour would pass before Ivy was required again. She turned away. All she wanted was water; she wondered where she might find the kitchen.

Moving out of the huge ballroom and through the center hall, Ivy followed a waitress weaving her way toward the back of the house into a lesser hall. Ivy made a quick sidestep to avoid a food trolley rolling out from the kitchen, causing her to bounce slightly against the doorjamb opposite. Another trolley followed. She edged back more firmly, and fell through.

"Whoa, there," murmured a bass voice behind her. One that sounded like rich fudge icing. A strong hand touched her shoulder, helping her to right herself. She glanced over her shoulder into chocolate brown eyes. Only this time they held no amusement. "Did you get lost?"

"Oh, um," she said, noticing the serious set of his mouth. He'd bathed and changed clothes, and his hair was still damp. "Noah something or other, isn't it?"

"Yeah, that's right. Noah."

"No, not really lost," she murmured, swinging about to glance at the second man in the room. Attractive, with deep blue eyes under a sunny swag of hair, he smiled a welcome. He wore light-brown casual trousers with a matching open-neck silk shirt.

He wasn't one of the guests; he must have something to do with the house or catering staff. She smiled in return. "I was looking for a glass of water and thought I'd find the kitchen. Sorry if I've intruded."

"No bother," he answered, snapping the door firmly closed before strolling to a tea trolley. Ice tinkled in the glass pitcher as he poured water into a tall glass. His smile grew inviting, a slight lifting of his lips giving his cheeks attractive dimples. "Here, have some from our tray. You might be knocked down out there. The service hallway is quite busy just now."

"That's very kind, thank you." She accepted the glass and sipped, casting a glance at the two men from beneath lowered lashes. From Noah, a quiet tension hung in the air, a feeling of something left unfinished. His hands, tightly fisted, were stuffed in his pockets.

She took in her surroundings. A library office, she thought, with a huge old library table desk of gleaming oak taking pride of place in front of a wall of books. Nearby a computer and stand looked more out of place than the wooden file cabinets in the corner, but a navy-blue sofa and matching chair brought the room back to a picture perfect library. On the whole the room was charming—but clearly a private one.

She had interrupted them.

Turning, she gazed hopefully at the three large windows that looked out on a terrace, but saw no door. Outside, a number of guests enjoyed the fine October weather. Deciding she needed to excuse herself as quickly as possible, she said, "Is there another way out of here? I'd just as soon avoid the heavy tide out there."

"Sorry, no," the blond man murmured. "But there's no need to hurry off. I'm Gerald Reeves, by the way." He gestured her toward the overstuffed chair. "Sit here a bit and catch your breath. The hallway should clear out soon. Unless the bride is looking for you?"

Noah remained silent, looking out the bank of windows.

"No, not at the moment," she answered, wondering what captured the gardener's attention outside, what caused his jaw to tense hard as granite.

She sat cautiously on the chair edge near the tea trolley, and switched her gaze toward the other man. "Reeves? Then this is your family home? I didn't realize anyone still maintained a residence here. And I have blundered into your private rooms. Oh, I'm so sorry."

"It's not an earth-shattering mix-up," Gerald reassured. "Could happen to anyone. It might put your mind more at ease to say we're friends." He raised a brow and let a slow smile creep across his face. "But I'd need to know your name."

"How remiss of me," she said with a chuckle, offering her hand to shake. "Ivy York, bridesmaid."

"Yes, so I see." He folded her hand in his for a proper moment before letting it go. "Friend or family?"

"A close friend."

Noah turned abruptly, and stalked toward the door. "Gotta get going. Nice to meet you again, Ivy. I'll have a couple of men clean up the garden tomorrow morning, Gerry."

Gerald's tone sharpened. "What about the lower grounds, Noah?"

At the door to the hall, Noah turned, his hand on the knob. "I'll, uh, be back in a couple of days to clean out the fish pond and winterize it. And I'll arrange for the tree trimmers to prune that eastern slope. The other matter..."

"Will take care of itself in due time," Gerald finished for him, leaning back lazily on the sofa. He smiled at Ivy, dismissing Noah.

"No doubt," Noah agreed with a note of sarcasm as he closed the door behind him.

Feeling even more like an interloper, Ivy sipped her water and allowed her gaze to roam the room again, taking in details she'd overlooked the first time. A sheaf of paperwork lay scattered across the desk and a stack of old wooden picture frames leaned against the desk leg. Even from yards away she knew they needed repair. Rising, she bent to examine them.

"These are beautiful," she murmured, looking at the worn gold leaf along the raised edges on the largest. "Eighteen-nineties to...maybe early twenties, aren't they?"

"Yes, that's right. How did you know?"

"It's my business to know," she said, glancing up. His gaze held interested surprise. "I deal with good framers, good suppliers. Um, are you looking for someone to repair these?"

"Actually, I hadn't yet thought about them much." He rose to stand nearby and stare at the frames. "I could always sell them, I suppose. Do you know of someone who specializes in repairing old wood?"

"Yes. Here," she grabbed a ballpoint from a holder and scribbled on a Post-it pad. "I'll give you his name. I think he can do a good job for you. Can't think of his phone number off the top of my head, but if you want to call my shop Monday, I can give it to you.''

''You own a shop, eh? What kind?''

''An interior design store, 'Wall's Intrigue', in Brookside.'' She set her glass on the tea trolley, and smiled. ''Thanks again, Mr. Reeves, for the water. But I really have to go back to the bride now, or they'll be sending out the bloodhounds in search for me.''

She slipped out into the almost empty service hall and from there into the main foyer, where the bride's sister caught up with her.

''There you are, Ivy,'' Kathy said, annoyed. ''Where have you been? We're wanted in the gazebo for pictures.''

''All right, I'm coming.''

Kathy didn't wait. She sailed forward through the milling crowd without looking back.

Following Kathy out a side door, Ivy headed across the lawn toward the white-columned structure set among maples, red oaks, dogwoods and redbud trees in autumn splendor. She paused to pull in a deep breath, letting the beauty flow through her; God really was the best decorator ever, she mused. Nothing could compare with the sight before her.

One of the groomsmen waved her to hurry. Hit with sudden exhilaration, Ivy picked up her skirt and sprinted down the gentle slope, her skirt billowing behind. A deep masculine laughter trailed her. She glanced over her shoulder, wondering at its source.

Noah Thornton. He stood in the half-shadowed doorway of a rear porch watching her. She couldn't imagine what about her amused him so, but she wouldn't let it bother her. Not a bit. After today, it was unlikely she'd ever see him again.

She ran faster. He laughed harder.

She refused to give him another glance.

Chapter Two

"Hello, can I help you?" Ivy asked, approaching the smartly dressed young woman who was examining a wall of original watercolors by a number of local artists Ivy supported. Her classic features and silky shoulder-length fall of blond hair looked familiar; Ivy tried to remember if they'd ever met. "If you're interested in one of these paintings, I can get it down for you."

"Those faces done in blues and mauves are interesting. Unusual—but no, I don't think so today," the woman replied before turning and studying her a moment. "I'm Barbara Reeves. You were at Reeves House the other day and offered to give my brother the number of a framer who specializes in repairing old picture frames?"

A group of three entered the shop, two women and a child. Saturdays in the old-fashioned Brookside shopping neighborhood were usually Ivy's busiest days and Tina had called in sick, leaving only Sherri and her to handle the crowd.

"Oh, yes." Now Ivy knew why the woman looked familiar. In addition to the resemblance to her brother, her picture had been in the papers a dozen times in the society columns. Barbara Reeves headed up several charity affairs every year. "I'll get it for you, but, um, can you wait a moment? My assistant is at lunch and I need to take care of the front counter."

Barbara shrugged and wandered to the finely carved wood mantelpieces on another wall. "I'm not in a rush. You really do have a lovely shop here. I'd no idea..."

The door dinged again as other customers entered. Ivy finished her transactions with the two young women, and turned to help the next when a pounding alerted her that someone wanted her attention at the shop's back door. Thankfully, Sherri, her most faithful help, returned just in time to answer it.

"Got a delivery," Ivy heard a deep voice pronounce. Instant recognition danced across her consciousness, and she almost tripped over her own feet to look into the back room.

"Sherri, I'll take care of this." She smiled at the customer, then glanced at Barbara Reeves apologetically, murmuring "A moment more, please," while she stepped into her crammed storage-cum-office area.

He looked bigger in the small room than he had outdoors. Taller and broader. At least he was neatly dressed in clean jeans and she had to admit the cherry-red shirt complemented his dark hair and eyes.

Holding a big cardboard box with the words Tomato Soup printed on its side atop his shoulder, he took time to look around with interest.

"Noah something, isn't it?" she murmured.

He brought his gaze around to look at her. His mouth curved into a half smile with a disarming charm of gentle flirtation. His eyes glinted with an expression clearly intent on letting her know he didn't believe her casual memory. "That's right."

Ivy pursed her mouth. She wouldn't let that smile get to her—even while those sparkling brown eyes gave her tummy a dip. What was he doing here?

"You work for a gardening business, don't you?"

"Something like that," he said, his smile widening. He seemed to think they shared a joke, as though they played a game. "Where do you want this stuff?"

"Wait a minute." She put up a defensive hand. Surely the man didn't think she'd called him in an attempt to see him again, did he? But his knowing expression said that was exactly what he thought. Well, she'd put a stop to that bit of nonsense right now.

"I don't recall ordering anything from you," she said distinctly as if speaking to a child. "I don't carry gardening equipment."

"Well, at least you remember my line of work," he replied, retaining a wry, teasing tone. He swung the box to the floor, taking up the three feet between them. "And like you, I own my business, The Old Garden Gate. Now, I have six outdoor wooden sculptures of trees and little critters for you. Great to hang on a porch wall or decorate a deck."

"I specialize in interiors."

He gave her a speculative look, causing her to smooth her hair behind one ear. "I sold one recently for a fireplace decoration."

"But I didn't order them," she insisted. "I wouldn't."

"Well, somebody ordered them. See?" He raised his brows and held out the small square of paper scribbled with the name of her shop and order. "Wall's Intrigue. Dated last Monday."

"Whose initials—" She glanced more closely at the carboned form and clamped her mouth shut. *A.A.* Aunt Arletta!

In any of her correspondence, notes, or gift tags to the family, her aunt never used her full name, Arletta York, she merely signed A.A. And here it was again. Surely Aunt Arletta wouldn't interfere in the shop's ordering lists again after Ivy scolded her for overflowing their supply of stained-glass bathroom wall fixtures?

The irrefutable evidence hung limply from between a masculine thumb and forefinger, waiting for her to accept it. Glancing into Noah's face, she clamped her teeth on a flare of high irritation. The man was right about one thing; her aunt had probably ordered the merchandise to bring Noah and Ivy together again. Throwing her at men's heads had become Aunt Arletta's latest hobby.

They were usually nice enough men. Ivy simply wasn't always enamored of Aunt Arletta's taste. Or her tactics.

That wasn't this man's fault, she admonished herself.

"All right," she said with a sigh. She might not like it, but she wouldn't embarrass her aunt or Noah by refusing to honor the order. Ivy did wonder how she could corral Arletta without deeply wounding her feelings. The shop's cash flow already ran closer to the zero line than was healthy. "Let's see your merchandise."

He bent to open the box, and brought out one of the objects for Ivy's inspection. To her surprise, it was a wood carving from a chunk of oak of two bear cubs climbing a pine tree. And it was good. The work showed more rough talent than training, but it had great appeal.

All business now, she said, "Let me see the rest."

Noah crouched down and pulled out the others—frogs and turtles, butterflies and birds, and dogwoods and tulips. Kneeling beside him, Ivy examined each one and glanced at Noah with renewed interest. "Did you do these?"

"Yeah, that one's mine." He stood and hung his thumbs from his jeans back pockets, watching her appraise the work. "A buddy and I do these in the winter when we don't have a lot else going on. He's the true artist, though. I just fill in my off-season time."

"Mmm..." She might have a few customers who would go for the primitive work. "It's the wrong season for most of these."

She stood also, and glanced around at her stuffed-to-the-ceiling shelves. "I'm setting out my holiday stock next week. Have you anything for the Thanksgiving and Christmas shoppers? I can use more Christmas stock. I already have enough wreaths coming in, but if you could come up with something different, something with a flair, bring it in. Meanwhile, I'll put out the bear and racoon and see what kind of interest it gets."

"Fair enough." He looked pleased. "Our outdoor

work has slowed down quite a bit. I'll talk to Matt and see what he suggests."

"I thought I heard a familiar voice back this way," Barbara Reeves said, ignoring the Private sign and pushing the door wider. "Noah, darling." The blonde's voice took on a near purr. "How are you? Haven't seen you in weeks. Where've you been keeping yourself?"

Noah dropped his hands to his sides. Ivy wouldn't have said he went on red alert, but she had a distinct impression of wariness.

"Hello, Barbara." He smiled vaguely. "I've been pretty busy."

"I called you last week," Barbara said, flipping her silky hair back with long, well-manicured fingers. "Didn't you get my message about the Shores' dinner?"

"Guess not. My phones were out for a couple of hours one day while the phone company did some work up the road."

"Well, I suppose that now your season has entered its resting phase, you'll have more time to accept my invitations," Barbara said with the familiarity of an old friend. "What about Saturday night?"

"Um..." He shifted his stance. "Have plans for Saturday."

"Too bad. Can't you break them?"

"Nope." His gaze grew determined, but his tone softened, as though letting her down easy. "Plans are solid."

Ivy felt she'd wandered into the middle of a twosome.

"Don't count on me to make the rounds of your social circuit this year, Barbara," Noah continued.

"My winter schedule may be different from the heavier seasons, but it's just as busy. In fact—" his glance touched Ivy with a spark of humor "—I've just joined a very active church where I expect to give quite a lot of my free time."

Which church? An instant suspicion tickled Ivy's spine. Was he talking about her church? Had Aunt Arletta done it again?

Aunt Arletta wasn't above a top-drawer selling job when it came to campaigning for Grace Community Church, and true enough, they carried several very active programs to service the community as well as three worship services on Sunday and several Bible studies and prayer meetings during the week. But she might just tie a knot in Aunt Arletta's panty hose if her aunt had been urging Noah to attend on her account.

"Ah, yes, soup kitchens and urchins, hmm?" Barbara said. "Well, perhaps another time. I have to run. Give me a call, Ms. York, when you have time to find that framer's number, will you?"

"Would you like me to call the framer for you?" Ivy responded.

"Sure, why not? Just let me know."

"I will. Thanks for coming in, Miss Reeves."

Ivy turned back to Noah. He shrugged, as though to suggest he had nothing to say about the encounter, and grinned. His dark eyes glinted with friendly humor.

"Now, about your merchandise," she said in a firm voice. "What kind of a price are you looking for?"

They wrapped up the business end of the transaction, then before Ivy could wonder whether he'd try to extend his contact with her or attempt anything close to a personal conversation, Noah said, "Nice doing business with you, Ivy. I'll leave through the store, if you don't mind. I can look around."

"Sure, help yourself." Leading the way, Ivy strolled back into the showroom.

Ivy turned her attention to a customer choosing wallpaper and matching drapes, and she became engrossed in color schemes and styles. Long moments later, a trill of laughter and a deep chuckle intruded upon her concentration.

Glancing toward the sound, she spotted Noah on a ladder removing one of her finest black walnut mantels from the wall display. Sherri waited at the ladder's base, her eyes alight with pleasure as she gazed up at Noah as though she were Juliet doing a reverse balcony scene with Romeo.

"Do you want to take this with you or have it delivered?" he asked the older woman waiting beside Sherri. Mrs. Gilliam, Ivy noted. A regular customer, she'd looked at the mantelpiece more than once but usually declared it too expensive.

"Oh, um, I have my van," the woman answered. "I'll take it now, if you'll carry it out for me."

"Be glad to, ma'am." Noah answered graciously. "Soon as Sherri rings you up, you just pull your van round back and I'll have this wrapped and ready to load. Do you have someone at home to unload it for you?'

"Ah, yes." The woman's salt-and-pepper head nodded, but her voice held an overtone of disappointment, as if hoping Noah might offer to deliver her purchase. "Yes, of course."

"Oh, thank you, Noah. I could never have taken

that down without you,'' Sherri gushed before turning to the customer. ''Will that be cash or charge, Mrs. Gilliam?''

''Charge, I suppose,'' Mrs. Gilliam said, running an appreciative hand along the dark polished wood. Intricately carved with racing horses, the heavy piece was the most expensive mantel in the shop. Ivy'd begun to think she'd never sell it without a drastic price reduction.

But Noah had. Her gaze followed him as he carried the object into the back room. Ivy finished with her own customer before stepping through the storeroom door.

''Got any real packing material back here?'' he asked her without looking her way as he searched a corner of the storeroom.

''The heavy-duty wrapping is behind the door over here.''

''Yeah, that's the stuff.'' He pulled the roll of batted paper out and hoisted it with ease onto the one counter Ivy kept clear for the purpose of wrapping large items. Having a person with muscle power about the store had its advantages, she admitted to herself. ''Wouldn't want to expose this thing to a possible scratch. About lost my back teeth when I heard Sherri quote the price.''

''Good work always commands a good price.''

''You know, this thing was so high up no one could see the delicate details,'' he said, looking it over carefully. ''Even needs a little dusting. I bet you could've sold it a lot faster if customers could see it better. Some of your wall could do with a rearrangement.''

"What's wrong with the wall?" He was right, but she was curious to know why he thought so.

"It's too random. Looks disorganized."

She blinked at his pointed reply. Obviously, subtlety wasn't one of his strong talents.

"That's because...because I don't have enough space to show like a gallery," she said, almost sputtering. Why she even thought she owed him an explanation was beyond her usual good sense. "I put up the work as it comes in."

Actually, she'd done that only in the last month. Usually she took time to reevaluate and rearrange the wall often.

"Looks like it, too. Might sell better if you group by color ranges. Or artists. You have three Burkes scattered over the wall that would show well together above one of the mantels."

"Only three? I thought I had two in one place and two in another."

"I sold one to that Ms. Reeves," Sherri said. "After she came out from talking to the two of you in the storeroom."

"Oh." Ivy glanced at the picture wall. Sure enough, an empty spot showed where the Burke that Barbara had bought once hung. "I'd be glad to rearrange your wall for you, if you'd like," Noah said. "I have a little time on my hands this week. No charge."

"I'll consider it," she answered. She knew the wall needed work; in truth, she'd been putting it off until Monday night after store hours when she planned to replace some of the art to show holiday wreaths. And with Aunt Arletta ordering things behind her back, and sometimes committing Ivy's time to help friends decorate with only thanks for compensation, she didn't need someone else handing out unsolicited advice.

A honk sounded beyond the outside rear door.

"Well, thanks for the help with Mrs. Gilliam's purchase," she said with sincerity, even though his critique of her shop's display area still rankled.

Yet he had been helpful, she reminded herself. She pulled the heavy door wide and struggled to be gracious as well as cooly professional. "It was kind of you. Here, I'll hold the door open."

"Glad to help." Halfway through the door, he paused. His dark eyes studied hers for half a second. "You've seen my work at Reeves house. Perhaps you'd consider carrying my card in your recommendation file. After coming to see my place, of course. Wouldn't expect you to tell your customers about my work unless I meet your standards."

"Right." That was really why he'd come today, she thought. She wouldn't admit to a tiny bit of disappointment that he hadn't come simply to see her again. Hidden agendas reminded her too much of Leon, the last man to whom she'd been engaged. Leon had wanted to control everything she did. He'd even had the nerve to fire her store assistant; that was the beginning of the end for Leon.

It was definitely the end of any remnant of her fantasy of a perfect marriage. Obviously this man had more depth to him than met the eye. But she'd never allow herself to become personally entangled with an overly controlling male again—ever.

"Send me a list of your services and prices and I'll give the idea some thought," she finally told Noah.

Yeah, right.

She didn't think so.

Several hours later as she slipped into the pew for the midweek prayer and praise service at church, she knew her wish to keep contact with Noah strictly on a professional basis was a vain one.

"Noah," Aunt Arletta greeted the young man enthusiastically. "I'm so happy to see you. Sit here with us."

"Thank you, ma'am. It's good to feel welcome."

Feeling like a grinch, Ivy scooted down the bench pew to make room for him. His smile was both genuine and sweet.

Hers felt more like a nervous rabbit's.

Chapter Three

Ivy dropped her keys on the kitchen counter of the apartment she shared with her aunt and sank into a chair. She let all her muscles relax. For the past week, with the exception of Sunday, she'd spent at least twelve hours a day at the store preparing for the approaching holiday shopping season. Last night she hadn't arrived home until midnight and she'd left again at seven this morning.

The day had been one ripe for a double headache.

One of her suppliers called with the news he'd be two weeks late with a Christmas delivery; a three-year-old child had tried climbing the shelf display then pitched a temper tantrum when she gently insisted he get down—without a mother in sight for a full five minutes; the man who cleaned her floor quit for greener pastures; and her feet hurt. After letting Sherri go home early, Ivy had stayed until almost seven. She wasn't even sure if the sun had made an appearance today. But at least her store was reasonably prepared for the holiday rush.

She sniffed. The fragrance of a chicken casserole filled her nostrils, making her tummy clench with hunger. What would she do without Aunt Arletta? she mused. Probably live on takeout. She hadn't taken time for lunch, either.

"Kind of late home, aren't you dear?" Her aunt popped into the kitchen and turned on the stove burner under the teakettle. "Well, never mind. You're just in time for a quick shower."

Shower? Her thoughts had run on the lovely image of a long soak in a bubble bath.

"What do you mean?" Ivy asked, knowing full well it meant her aunt probably wanted to go out somewhere. Couldn't be grocery shopping—she'd done that last night. She frowned. No, that had been three nights ago. Maybe she had a meeting of some church committee.

Ivy hoped it meant her aunt only needed a ride somewhere and not Ivy's company for the evening. After talking with customers all day, she was too tired to even crack a smile. "It's Tuesday."

"Ah, yes. Tuesday." Aunt Arletta met with a seniors group for Bible study and dessert on Tuesday afternoons, which usually satisfied her craving for company—at least for that day. On Tuesday evenings, they stayed at home.

Not for the first time Ivy wished her aunt had learned to drive. The fact she hadn't had caused Ivy and her mother, Brenda, more than one problem while Ivy was growing up. Aunt Arletta didn't think anything of making plans without consulting anyone else first, but she was such a dear and contributed so much to other people's comfort, Ivy never had the heart to refuse her. It hadn't been so bad before her dad died; she was his aunt, after all. He cheerfully ran errands for Aunt Arletta or drove her to wherever she needed to go.

Ivy shifted from her outer wrap and let her head drop back to rest against the chair. Closing her eyes for a moment, she pulled up memories of her dad—something she often did when she felt tired or down.

Jonathan York had been of average size, but Ivy had thought him tall enough to touch the ceiling. They'd ridden bikes together, shoveled snow and made snow forts all winter, roller-skated in the hot summer evenings, jaunted down the sidewalks side by side every Saturday morning on their way to shop. They munched on donuts while strolling home, a bag of groceries in each of their arms, and he'd simply grin widely at her mother's scold over spoiling her. She'd been her daddy's girl and she'd adored him. No one would ever mistake her for anyone else's child, her mother said frequently, with their matching coppery curls and hazel green eyes.

Without realizing it, Ivy sighed. She still missed him dreadfully. When her father died of sudden heart failure, she'd just turned fourteen. She thought her world had stopped, and in a way, it had. Things changed rapidly for her and her mother afterward; although they'd never had much in earthly goods, their life became even leaner. Bless Aunt Arletta. They never would have made it if she had not moved in with them, throwing her own small income and nurturing instincts into the family pot.

It was Aunt Arletta who had taught her about her heavenly Father. And how to talk with Him and what the scriptures said of Him.

Aunt Arletta did a lot for the family, but she never

learned to drive. They'd had the old car, then, already four years old when her dad died, and her mom took over the duties of ferrying the family. But they soon found that balancing the various needs was often difficult; taking the bus hadn't always fit Ivy's schedule or routes, and cabs were too expensive. Too proud, her mother refused to ask for help from anyone besides Aunt Arletta. They couldn't always depend on someone else to cart one of them around, her mom had said. They just had to "make do".

Ivy was usually the one who made do. If she hadn't a ride to somewhere, she walked. She walked almost everywhere as a teen.

Ivy'd learned a great deal about personally making do. She made her choices of clothing and activity do triple duty, and budgeted her time and money with care, even while lavishing her time on learning all she could about fine furnishings, color palettes and design. The contrast between the exquisite furniture, fine art and carefully designed interiors she studied and the reality of their humble apartment made a deep impression on her, and she'd determined even then to have a better home one day.

She took her first part-time job at a department store the month she turned fifteen and a half. During college, she switched to an upscale furniture store and juggled full-time hours with school. She socked away every penny she could, waiting for the day when she could invest it.

She and Aunt Arletta, since her mother remarried and moved out west, still made do with their small apartment and frugal budget while she poured all her profits back into the store. But one day she'd have a big house and more than one new car. If their Christmas season was good, this was the year Wall's Intrigue would more than break even. Someday, Ivy dreamed now, she'd have money enough to buy a brand-new car right off the dealer's lot and take Aunt Arletta on a long driving vacation.

"So what's going on?" She let her daydreams go with a sigh.

"We have a guest coming to dinner."

"Okay." She didn't bother to ask who. Aunt Arletta frequently asked her friend, Shirley, who lived two doors away to a meal. "What's it being Tuesday to do with it?"

"Well, tomorrow is your light day."

"Mmm..." Ivy closed at four on Wednesdays, but starting next week she'd begin her holiday hours when they'd be open until eight every night except Sunday when she closed the store entirely. "You haven't set the table yet. Want me to do it?"

"No, dear. You run along and have your shower. Oh, and Kelly called a few moments ago."

"They're back?" Ivy scrambled out of her chair and headed down the hall to her tiny bedroom where she could return a call in peace. Two weeks without talking to her best friend left her with a hole to fill. Their friendship would be different now; marriage always changed loyalties and priorities. Rightly so, she'd told herself over the years as one by one her friends had entered into that state. But she and Kelly had been the last holdouts in their crowd and had made solemn vows they wouldn't let marriage put distance in their friendship. Even so, Ivy mused, she wouldn't see as much of her friend from now on. It was the way of things.

She punched Kelly's number and spent a pleasant

thirty minutes listening to how wonderful Hawaii had been for a honeymoon.

"Ivy, are you almost ready for dinner?" Aunt Arletta called.

"Five minutes, Aunt A."

Showering quickly, she also shampooed her auburn curls. She gave her hair a halfhearted swipe with the towel, then decided to let it dry naturally. Rummaging through her closet, she grumbled about having to dress again at all. She'd much rather wear her pj's and robe. She'd likely pass out as soon as supper was over anyway.

At the bottom of her chest, she found a loose navy sweat outfit and pulled it on. Shirley wouldn't care what Ivy wore.

"...and Ivy opened her store three years ago. She inherited her father's creativity, you see," her aunt's gentle voice murmured through the hall as Ivy sauntered down it in stockinged feet. "But she never could focus in a single direction, poor dear. So the interior design store gives her enough variety—"

Not focus? Aunt A never understood her occasional interest in architecture or how the two areas of design interacted.

Whoever her aunt was talking to, it wasn't Shirley. Ivy reached the kitchen door and stopped cold. Her aunt's small plump figure stirred a pot on the stove while a tall, athletic one filled three glasses with milk.

"Hi, Ivy. It's about time you got out of that shower," Noah said as though his presence in her kitchen were quite a normal occasion. His gaze swept over her face, free of makeup, and noted her still-damp hair, minus its usual smooth fall. "We're starved."

"Yes, we certainly are. And you must be as well. Sit down, children. Soup first. Then a nice chicken-and-noodle casserole."

"Noah!" She ignored her aunt's direction entirely, trying not to let her mouth drop open like a buffoon. "Why are you here?"

"Taking shameless advantage of your aunt's generous invitation," he said, hooking a foot around a chair leg to bring it out from under the table. He appeared completely at home in her small kitchen, and wonderfully comfortable with Aunt Arletta. "She asked me the other day after I agreed to chauffeur some seniors on an outing. We're making it a weekly adventure."

"What?" Heart beating with sudden suspicions, she licked her lips to ask calmly, "What are you making a weekly adventure?"

"Our outings," Aunt Arletta answered with delight. Ivy let her breath out, thinking herself almost too foolish to have thought her aunt meant she'd invited Noah for a weekly dinner.

Yet, knowing her aunt, the idea wasn't so far-fetched. She continued to listen to her aunt's explanation, trying not to stare or be taken in by Noah's handsome face.

"Noah's agreed to play chauffeur and escort for the senior outings until spring. We had sixteen of us today, and having a nice young man like Noah to assist some of us into the bus was a pleasure. He took us right to the back of the Thomas Hart Benton House so that no one had to go up those steps. Used the ramps for the two in wheelchairs so all of us could go. Even old Robert Dearborn was pleased, and you know how crabby Robert can be.''

Ivy blinked. Noah touched her shoulder, reminding her to sit. Sinking into the chair, she narrowed her eyes at him slightly; no one could be that perfect.

Considerate and generous to older people and functioned well in a kitchen? What was he up to? What did he want? He'd only joined the church a week or two ago. He'd sat nearby during the worship service. While always polite, Ivy'd never encouraged his interest by one single eyelash sweep.

He caught her suspicious gaze and gave her a silent shrug while his mouth spread into a half smile, his eyes glowing with personal invitation. Come and see, he seemed to beckon. Come on, I'm harmless.

She could almost fall into those warm eyes, sweet as molasses.

''Noah, we'd be pleased if you offered thanks for our supper,'' Aunt Arletta suggested. ''We so seldom have men guests around our table these days. Not since Ivy broke her engagement to that—''

''Aunt A!''

''All right, all right. But it's true.'' Aunt Arletta's eyes weren't a bit repentant. ''We don't have men guests these days. Personally, I'd like to hear a man's prayer of thanks.''

''I'm honored, ma'am.'' Reverence replaced his gentle teasing as Noah bowed his head. ''Lord, we are deeply grateful for your bounty here in this kitchen, and for friends and life. We thank you for this meal and the hands that prepared it. We ask you to bless each of us and the evening ahead with your favor. Amen.''

Ivy blinked at the sincerity she heard in Noah's

voice. Did he really know the Lord so well? She'd met a few men who pretended far more piety than they really felt. Later actions gave her reason to question if even their basic faith was a lie. Like Leon.

She'd thought Leon perfect at first. An ambitious lawyer, he belonged to a wealthy, high-profile church. His faithful church attendance and involvement in the church's finance committee impressed her. Everything looked bright between them.

She soon found his controlling nature to be obsessive. When she pointed that out to him, he couldn't see it as wrong. The final break came when he wanted to delegate Aunt Arletta to a home. Any home other than his. He had no room in his life for a dotty old lady, he'd told Ivy, and neither would she after they married. That particular wedding dress she'd packed away without a single pang of what-might-have-beens.

Ivy let her aunt and Noah carry the conversation and listened with only half an ear as they discussed the day's events.

"And how is the holiday season shaping up for you, dear?" her aunt said, finally noticing her silence.

"Earl quit today," she said, chewing slowly on a piece of bread. She wondered how long she could let the floor go before she had to tackle it herself. "Said he had a full-time job elsewhere and wouldn't have time for me anymore."

"Oh. Well, you'll find somebody else to do your floors."

"Floors?" Noah said, dipping a second portion of chicken and noodles onto his plate. "I know someone who's looking for a part-time job. A college kid.

Works for me in the summer, mowing lawns and such. Brad could help with your wall displays, too.''

''I've been managing my wall displays all right up 'til now,'' she stated, pressing her lips together. Sort of. She'd hired a man to hang those heavy mantels.

''Sure you have. And that's why you don't change the display as often as is needed. Is it really wise to try to handle something beyond your physical strength?''

'''Blessed is the man who finds wisdom...''' Aunt Arletta quoted.

'''Wisdom is supreme; therefore get wisdom,''' Noah responded with his own Proverbs quote, and a quick smile for the older woman before turning back to Ivy. ''How about young Brad? Are you willing to train him?''

Ivy let go of her pride and glanced at Noah hopefully. ''He's not looking for just a Christmas job, is he? I need someone every week.''

''I think it's safe to say he'd stay with you 'til spring, at least.''

''All right. Send him around and I'll talk to him. Thanks, Noah.'' Ivy smiled into his eyes, her gratitude for his help making her forget all about ulterior motives. Right now, she'd take whatever help came her way.

And she was simply too tired to fight the attractive buzz Noah's brown eyes gave her. Eyes that made her want to put her head on his strong shoulder and sigh.

She'd have to watch that, she told herself. Falling too easily for a charming man had been her downfall the first year in college.

Dan was gorgeous, with long dark lashes any

woman would envy, and a romantic nature that swept her off her feet. After only two months of seeing each other, they become engaged, planning a perfect future life together. Ivy's head drifted with the clouds as she chose her wedding dress and four bridesmaids' dresses. She worked extra hours and even went without meals to pay for them as they waited in layaway for her wedding day.

Ivy had been so wrapped in the throes of idealized love, she'd failed to recognize how easily Dan spread his charm. Two weeks before she was to meet his parents, she unexpectedly found a stack of letters, current ones, from a girl back in his Texas hometown. That girl was engaged to Dan, *too.*

Brokenhearted, Ivy let Dan go back to his Texas girl and packed away her dreams along with her wedding clothes. Her easy trust went with them.

Now she searched for a man who had more to offer than mere charm and good looks. She wanted a man of substance. A sophisticated, polished man who could offer her an easier life-style than what she'd known up until now. She'd settle for no less.

"Well, ladies," Noah said half an hour later, picking up plates and carrying them to the sink. "I hate to eat and run, but I do have some work to take care of in the morning. Thanks, Arletta. That was a wonderful meal."

"Really, Noah, you don't have to help with the dishes," Aunt Arletta replied with almost a simper. "It's my pleasure to have someone to cook for now and again. Does my ego good, you know."

"Well, thanks a bunch, Aunt A. Don't I count?"

"Of course you do, Ivy dear, but one likes cooking

for a healthy appetite sometimes. Half the time, you don't even eat."

"I'll be glad to pander to your pleasure in cooking anytime you say the word, Arletta. Well, I'll say good-night now." He paused to give Ivy a considering stare, his thumbs hooked in his back pockets. "Ivy, I think you need to get a good night's sleep. You're lovely as always, but looking a little worn-out. Don't work too hard."

He left then, swinging out of the door without giving her a chance at a comeback. She stood a moment counting to ten, wondering if he was worth even that high a number before stomping off the bed.

Chapter Four

Gerald Reeves called Wall's Intrigue the next day.

"Oh, Yes, Mr. Reeves, I called the framer, Joe Barton," Ivy answered in the pleasant, professional voice she'd learned at sixteen. "He suggested you have someone bring the frames into his shop. Didn't you receive the message I left on your machine?"

"Yes, I have it. And since Mr. Barton is also an art restorer, I've asked him to come to the house to check the conditions of our older paintings. But I'd like you to come as well, if you don't mind, and give me an opinion of what we might do in an upstairs hall and a couple of rooms I'm thinking of redecorating. I'll pay the going rate for your time, naturally."

"Of course I'd be happy to," she replied, a little surprised and flattered, too. If Gerald Reeves wanted to hire her, it meant her store had gained a notch in reputation.

She hadn't done much in the way of home calls in her consulting work until now—the store kept her too busy. She did keep a list of interior designers for that purpose, two of whom had excellent reputations, and offered to call either of them now.

"No, I'll be quite satisfied with your services, Ivy. And call me Gerry, please? See you Friday at eleven," he said, not giving her a chance to say no.

"Yes, that will do nicely."

Ivy hung up the phone and happily picked up the work roster to make sure she had enough help in the store on Friday. Sherri was scheduled to work Friday evening, she recalled. She really couldn't ask her to work all day and evening, too.

That meant she'd have to make do with Tina, who was inexperienced and new. But she couldn't leave Tina alone; the girl was too nervous. Too many things could go wrong. Especially now that the year's busiest season was getting under way.

Yet she couldn't miss this opportunity to work on Reeves House. It could mean a lot in future recommendations.

She sighed and straightened her shoulders. Keeping good help with only part-timers always meant a juggling of schedules; she sometimes bent herself into a pretzel to keep a reliable clerk. She appreciated Sherri, who worked on a small commission above her minimum salary. Ivy considered her worth every penny, but the store profits simply wouldn't stretch to offering that kind of arrangement to another clerk.

Tapping her pen against her notepad, she wondered if she should hire the busy mother who applied for work last week. Emily only wanted to work through the holidays. Emily had retail experience, but she'd have to find a baby-sitter if she worked days, she'd said.

Perhaps Aunt Arietta...

No, no, no! For heaven's sake, what was she thinking? The last time she'd asked Aunt A to watch the store for a morning the older woman sold an expensive window treatment for half price and Ivy'd had to pay for the installation, as well. All because Aunt A had read the price chart wrong. Not wanting to give the shop a bad name, Ivy hadn't felt it was good business to try to correct the mistake with the customer.

There was always the college kid Noah recommended. Without giving herself time to think about it, she looked up Noah's number.

"Morning, Old Garden Gate," his deep voice rumbled out, sending a current of warmth right through the line. Every time she heard his voice, Ivy wondered if it made other women feel like warm syrup ran through their veins, too.

"Hello, Noah," she said in her business voice while tamping down a desire to soften her response. "This is Ivy. I called for the number of the young man you suggested might be interested in working for me."

"Ah, yes. Brad. Just a moment." She heard a bit of paper shuffling before he gave her the numbers, then said, "He's probably in class this morning, though."

"All right." She tapped her pen and circled the number. "Thanks. I appreciate it."

That was easy enough. She didn't have to engage him in more talk. A business call didn't have to extend to anything personal.

"Ivy?"

"Yes?"

"There's a single's potluck on Saturday night at church. You going?"

The singles from church gathered together for social purposes on a regular basis. His invitation sounded too general. Why should she jump to go? "Oh, I don't know. Usually I'm pretty ragged out by Saturday night."

"C'mon." His tone took on one of a coaxing big brother—but the melting inside her heated up just the same. "You have to have a little fun now and again and you close at six on Saturdays. When was the last time you just relaxed with a group of people your own age? And it's usually a good-size group, I'm told, and I'm new to this bunch."

Uh-huh. Right. As though he'd ever feel a stranger in any gathering.

"I'll see how I feel on Saturday."

"You could make me feel at home." The invitation, spoken in a deeper voice, made her heart skip a beat. There wasn't anything brotherly about it.

"Well, maybe."

Now why had she gone and said that?

"Good." His tone changed from coaxing to commanding. "I'll pick you up around half past seven. Meanwhile, if Brad doesn't work out for you, let me know. I might have someone else who could help you out."

Uh-huh. Right. Since when was he her employment agency?

She left a message on Brad's answering machine and went back to checking over her work applications. The young mother, Emily, was her best choice after all.

On Friday morning, she left a nervous Tina and

Emily in charge of the noontime walk-in trade, and giving a silent prayer that all would go smoothly in her absence, left for Reeves House. Brad would come later in the afternoon to work with Sherri. She could trust Sherri to train him. And she'd be there until closing herself, and could observe how the young man worked out.

At Reeves House, a brown-haired young woman answered the huge old oak door, a duster in hand.

"Hello, I'm Ivy York," Ivy announced. "I've come to see Gerry."

"I'm right here, Ivy," Gerry said, smiling at her as he appeared from the hall's interior. His glance at her curvy figure, dressed in a cinnamon-brown-colored business suit that nearly matched her hair, was openly appreciative. Warming, she returned his smile.

"Thanks, Cam." He spoke smoothly in a practiced manner, and gave the girl an impersonal nod. "Joe Barton is just arriving, I believe. Let him in, please, and show him back to the office."

Turning, he led Ivy to the library room where they'd first met. Picking up a bone china coffee mug, he asked, "Coffee first or after we conclude our tour?"

"Afterward, I think. I'd like to get started."

"Fair enough. I have a long hall on the third floor that's rather dark and definitely plain, and four bedrooms there. After we finish with Joe, I'd like you to view them. Haven't thought about fixing up the top floor before now because we really don't use it. It was originally intended to house the servants, but times being what they are, we don't employ full-time housemaids and such anymore."

"I would think a house this size needed full-time care," she murmured.

"Oh, it does, indeed, and careful attention to upkeep, as well." Gerry brushed his hair from his eyes and glanced around him as though considering her thought. "But most of it is farmed out to companies who specialize in services. Some with long-standing associations with Reeves House, of course. But only an older couple live in full-time, the Marshalls. They have an apartment off the kitchen. Grace cooks if either Barbara or I want a meal at home, and Tom assists wherever he's needed.

"But we have a completely different crew when entertaining at Reeves House or leasing it out. We contract a catering company, a party planning service, and landscape company, of course, all of which take care of needed details to keep the old place in show condition. But we've had occasions when we've been asked to rent the entire house for a period of time, you know, like a house party or small company retreat, and Barbara thinks it's time to consider the idea of redoing the top floor."

"In here, Mr. Barton," the young house duster said. She disappeared again and Joe, middle-aged and paunchy, appeared in her place. Ivy made introductions.

"Let's go, then," Gerry said, directing them back into the main hall. "I've several pieces of original art that need cleaning, and quite a few old frames need both cleaning and repair. I considered having the Nelson Gallery experts look at them, but when Ivy told me she had someone she trusted to look after them, I decided on you."

"Then you'll be happy to know I'm registered

with the Nelson and the Art Institute,'' Joe responded.

''Good. I had a feeling Ivy only dealt with the best,'' Gerry answered, a grin tugging at his mouth while his blue eyes threw her the compliment intended in his comment.

They began with the first-floor library, studying the old paintings that had hung without disturbance for half a century. Ivy recognized several paintings by local artists from past generations, two of which she thought quite valuable, and a few others of very good quality.

''I've a print of this one,'' Ivy remarked in surprise. ''I didn't realize the original was in a private collection.''

''My great-grandfather believed in supporting the local talent, as you can see,'' Gerry replied. ''When he inherited the house, he trotted out his collection for display.''

Joe gave his suggestions as they proceeded into the formal parlor, through the huge dining room, the large ballroom where the wedding had been held, and up the long stairway. Along the way, Ivy glanced at the furnishings, recognizing various styles of mixed generations. On the second floor, where the principal bedrooms surrounded a comfortable-looking informal lounge, they viewed half a dozen lesser artists.

''That takes care of the lot on display,'' Gerry said. ''You can start after the first of the year. The house is in use most of December.''

Barbara joined them as they concluded. ''Oh, hello, Ivy. My goodness, yes. We are hosting a major charity do the first week in December, and three weddings before Christmas. A body can scarcely call her home her own anymore."

"Now, Barb, it isn't that bad. Besides, we have all of January to ourselves. Do you want to come along to hear what Ivy may do with the top floor?"

"Oh, I suppose. Otherwise, my dearest brother, you might choose to paint it all in circus colors."

Gerry laughed at his sister's sally and took Ivy's elbow to guide her back through the hall.

Joe excused himself and left, and they climbed to the third floor. Ivy studied the four bedrooms, ideas flowing like a steady breeze, and gave a couple of spontaneous suggestions. Chatting about ideas to cheer the dark rooms, they returned to the first floor.

Ivy glanced at her watch. Almost one.

"Well, that took longer than I'd imagined," Gerry said. He reached for the thermos coffee keeper, then put it down again. "Won't you stay for lunch?"

The invitation caught Ivy by surprise. Social engagements with customers didn't usually come out of her kind of business. "Why, that sounds very nice, but I really need to return to the store. I have a new clerk who can only work until two."

"How disappointing," Barbara murmured, flipping her lovely hair behind her shoulder. Ivy envied that sleek, sophisticated look that only a steady visit to a beauty salon could produce. Other than a good cut every six weeks, she usually took care of her own hair.

"Well," Ivy said, picking up her purse from a side table. "I'll put some of the ideas we discussed in writing, along with estimates of the costs and a time frame for the work. I should have it ready by the first week in January."

"Sounds great." Gerry said. "Come on, it's raining. I'll walk you to your car."

He grabbed an umbrella from a brass container near the front stairway. Outside, he opened the car door for her, but held it open after she slid inside, his gaze taking on a personal appeal.

"I have a committee dinner thing tonight. Boring as blue Monday. Wouldn't be if you'd come with me."

"Why, Gerry, that's sweet of you to say," she said, surprised again, reassessing what she saw in his eyes. He'd really meant his invitation to lunch. "But I have to work until eight, when I close the store, and it usually takes me another thirty minutes to wrap up."

"Oh, well." He let his disappointment show, then brightened. "But we can salvage the evening if you'll let me take you out for dessert afterward. And it'll give me an excuse to leave the meeting early."

She considered it a moment. Dating a client wasn't exactly good policy. And two dates on the same weekend? She hadn't had so much male attention in months.

But one invitation came from exactly the kind of man she'd been looking to meet. Gerry had charm, social polish, a prominent family background and wealth. She warmed to the idea.

"That does sound nice. All right."

Ivy arrived at the store just in time for Aunt Arletta's visit, her friend Shirley in tow. She didn't have to wonder how they'd got there. The church's gray van took up a prime parking spot just in front of Wall's Intrigue and Noah strolled in behind the two.

"Noah agreed to help the seniors shop once a

week until after Christmas,'' Aunt Arletta said. ''The others went to poke around the other shops, but I told Shirley you had just the right thing for her sister's birthday. And at a reasonable price.''

''Sure, Aunt Arletta,'' Ivy told her, knowing her aunt intended for her friend to gain a healthy discount. Ivy didn't mind that much; she liked occasionally indulging her aunt's generosity, and Shirley had certainly filled many a lonely hour for Aunt A. But she sincerely hoped the holiday seasonal buying would make up for all the times her aunt had offered ''reasonable prices'' to her friends.

''Ask Emily to help you,'' she whispered near her aunt's ear. ''She's new just this morning. Then you can evaluate how well she relates with customers.''

''Oh. Well, of course, dear. Shirley, come look at these lovely candlesticks.''

''Wall sconces,'' Ivy said under her breath as her aunt moved away. She began to straighten a cluttered display of tiny ceramic carolers near the checkout counter.

''They're still candlesticks,'' Noah said low.

Ivy glanced over her shoulder, catching the teasing glint in Noah's eye. One edge of his mouth twitched.

She sighed. He would be picky about exact descriptions. In fact, she could think of several annoying traits she was learning about Noah Thornton. ''They're electric lights in the appearance of brass candlesticks.''

'''An honest answer is like a kiss on the lips,''' he replied, his tone low and velvety. His words evoked in her a sudden reminder of how attractive he was, and she briefly wondered what it might be like to kiss a gardener.

"Proverbs 24, verse 26." Aunt Arletta's voice rang out from across the way, effectively bringing Ivy's wandering thoughts back with a jolt. Aunt Arletta heard anything quoted from Scripture.

"Right," he said, raising his voice to carry, then proceeded to nod and smile to the other two customers who glanced their way.

Ivy went to offer them assistance, deciding she could do without this entanglement during working hours. But the natural avoidance only lasted long enough for her to ring up their purchases. Noah hung around the checkout counter, picking up and putting down a trio of ceramic angels.

"I'll take these, Ivy, if you please," Shirley said in her shy way as she handed her the wall sconces. "They're just perfect for my sister's birthday and Christmas gift combined. She'll love them."

"Glad you found what you wanted, Shirley." Ivy quoted an amply reduced price as she packed them into a gift box.

"Oh, but the price sticker says..." Shirley's faded eyes went round with happy surprise which Ivy felt more than made up for her lost profits.

"Yes, I know. But you see, I've had those in the store for months now and it's time I turned over the stock. Cash flow, you know," Ivy insisted staunchly. "I'm just happy you like them."

"Well, in that case, if you're sure," Shirley murmured tentatively.

Behind Shirley, Aunt Arletta smiled with a pleased nod.

From the corner of her eye, Ivy caught Noah's musing glance of approval.

What? Just because she wanted to make a decent

living and an occasional profit as well, even hoped to make her store really successful, she couldn't be generous when a little charity was in order? So she'd fibbed just a bit. Those candlesticks would have eventually sold at the retail price, but Ivy knew how tight Shirley's budget was, knew she lived on a fixed income just as Aunt Arletta did. She also knew when not to call her generosity by the name of charity.

Did that mean her answer no longer merited a kiss?

Shocked at her own shot of disappointment at the unbidden thought, she quickly glanced away.

Moments later, Noah's silent response, given swiftly as they left the store, glinted from half-closed lids. His brown eyes made her a promise. A promise Ivy felt all the way to her toes.

About ten minutes before closing, Ivy glanced up and spotted Gerald pausing to gaze at her window display. He wore a camel-colored cashmere topcoat, and his hair gleamed like spun gold in the streetlight.

Like his sister, once he came inside, he gravitated toward the artists' wall and studied the work Ivy featured. He was used to viewing the finer art galleries with their high price tags, she was certain, while her artists were still struggling to make a name for themselves. Covertly, she studied his expression for a reaction.

Ivy strolled to stand beside him. "Hi."

He turned and smiled beguilingly as though he knew it was she. As if he were used to being admired.

"Hi, yourself. My meeting turned out shorter than I anticipated." He glanced around the store, empty now except for Sherri. "Any chance you can get out of here early?"

"Oh..." She thought of all she needed to do to wrap up the closing. Straightening the counter displays could wait until Monday morning, and Brad already waited in the back room to clean the floors. She supposed she could speed up her day's receipt count, but she still had to drop her deposit in the bank.

"Thirty minutes, Gerry. Sorry, but a working girl has to pay attention to her p's and q's. Why don't I meet you at Barlow's? They're open 'til ten."

He shrugged. "All right, if you must."

Ivy pushed to close the store. Exactly twenty-five minutes later, Ivy slid into a booth across from Gerry. The impatience he wore left the moment she sat down.

"Ah, there you are. Thought you'd be forever."

Smiling, she let his flattering gaze soothe her nagging guilt at leaving too much work undone. "I came as quickly as possible."

"You have a nice little shop, Ivy. But I'm sure much of what you do can be delegated to your employees. That's what you have them for, you know."

"Mmm... Well, I'm here now." Ivy smiled at him and the smile he gave her in return made her pulse quicken.

Yes, Gerry Reeves was *exactly* the type of man she'd been looking for.

Chapter Five

The monthly potluck had been pronounced kick-back time for busy people, Noah'd been told. No one dressed up for these events. Jeans and sneakers, or something equally comfortable was the dress code. Nevertheless, he'd bought new sneakers for the occasion, pulled out his favorite college T-shirt, and even made an effort to press his best flannel shirt to wear over it. He hadn't had this kind of a date in a long time.

Ivy looked about sixteen wearing a faded blue T-shirt and jeans when she met him at the apartment door, ready to go and carrying a covered cake plate. She answered, "Aunt Arletta" when he raised a questioning brow.

He led her to his freshly washed red pickup and opened the wide passenger door. She shot him an unreadable glance and shifted the cake and her purse before grabbing the doorframe. He put a hand to her elbow and lifted. She was light on her feet and slid gracefully onto the bench seat—but she didn't go very far over toward the driver's side.

Letting his breath out slowly, Noah wondered what it would take to make Ivy feel more cozy toward him. Nothing about their friendship so far had given him any encouragement toward thinking she might fall for him in any big way. If his gut instinct hadn't told him better, he'd say she was attracted but fighting to keep acres of distance between them.

She made small talk on the ten-minute drive to the church. Or rather, he made idle comments on the weather or local events while she answered politely but without much interest. It seemed her thoughts were elsewhere.

They arrived just in time to join the circle of about thirty people, mixed singles who met once a month for fellowship and sustenance, both spiritual and mundane, as they laid a table groaning with combined food. Aunt Arletta had told him about the group. More women than men, it contained the never-marrieds and widowed, but also the divorced singles, all of whom had left their first blush of youth behind them. They used the group to fill in the gaps of their lives, shared prayers, and frequently helped each other out on a personal level, as well. According to Arletta's comments, this bunch offered comradery with an open heart.

He hoped so, because he sorely needed a new set of friends.

As soon as the evening prayer had been given in the church multipurpose room, Ivy slid into a chair opposite two core members of the thirty-something singles, Haley and Donna. Noah took the chair beside her.

"Hi, everyone," she said, picking up a chicken leg from her plate. "This is Noah Thornton. He's new to the church and looking for friends, so make him feel at home, people. I hear he plays a mean basketball game."

Noah slanted her a look, then nodded to the two women opposite them when they greeted him. Yeah, he did need friends, especially ones who shared the same faith and values, but he'd hoped Ivy...

"Where did you hear that?" he asked her between bites of scalloped potatoes.

"Aunt A, of course. Need you ask?"

"Guess not." He bit into a hard roll. "She does spread the news, doesn't she?"

"Basketball is your game, is it?" Haley asked.

"I play for a little fun now and again."

"Ever play in school?" she queried.

He chewed thoughtfully a moment while he returned Haley's steady gaze. It carried a glint of challenge. He'd loved the game in high school, had even counted himself as one of his team's star players, much to his dad's delight. He hadn't been half-bad on his West Coast college team, either, but not good enough to make the pros if he'd wanted. It hadn't been much of a disappointment to him, even though his dad had hoped for more, because Noah already knew he wanted a somewhat quieter life than a pro athlete's would bring.

But surely no one here in the Midwest would know about his near star ability. He kept his skill reasonably sharp with a hoop set up near his trailer on the edge of his nursery fields and played with the fellows who worked with him. Hands down, he beat them every time. But he had no regrets about refusing to push into the pros or choosing his quieter profession.

He glanced again at Ivy. Something told him he'd confessed more than he should have when he and Arletta got to talking the other day on the way home from shopping. How much had he really told the old lady? Or more to the point, what had she told Ivy?

"A bit," he finally conceded to Haley's question.

"Care to play after dinner?" came the careless offer. He recognized an underplayed challenge when he heard one.

"Guess we could." His gaze roamed the gymlike room and spotted the goals at each end. Of course! The church was large enough to provide for all kinds of activities.

He carefully assessed Haley's narrow-eyed green gaze, her slender, wiry figure, and guessed her to be a player. About thirty, he thought, but a woman who kept in shape. Then he turned to Ivy's profile, idly noticing a few freckles across her nose. She didn't have the athlete's build, but he thought her curvy femininity very appealing.

"Anyone else here up to it?" he asked, a grin tugging his mouth. He had the feeling he'd been set up, but if this crowd wanted to play, he was game. He wished he'd brought his gym shorts, though.

"Hey Scotty!" Haley shouted. "You up for basketball?"

"Sure, you bet!" came the reply.

A couple wearing forest-green matching T-shirts, whom Ivy addressed as Kelly and Scott, joined the table.

"They're the bride and groom who married that day at Reeves House," she explained. "Technically—" she gave a pointedly teasing stare at her friend "—they don't belong in this group anymore, now that they're married. Why aren't the two of you home cooing and cuddling?"

"C'mon, Ivy, just because we're married now doesn't mean we've suddenly gotten stodgy and dull overnight," Kelly said with a laugh. "What—you want to banish us now?"

"Naw, we won't let you desert us," Haley insisted. "I don't care if you're married or not. I have to beat Scotty at least once in this century."

"Huh," Scott grunted. "You wish! It's a shame when a female basketball coach can't stand up to a little local competition."

"Well, Noah, here, is panting for a little activity," Ivy offered. Then lowering her tone, she said for his benefit, "Haley and Scott are brother and sister, if you hadn't noticed."

Chewing thoughtfully, Noah studied Ivy's face from beneath half-lowered lashes. A teasing spark shone from her deep blue-green gaze, though no hint of a smile captured her mouth.

"Well?" Haley demanded.

"D'you play?" Noah asked Ivy, recognizing he had been caught in a friendly long-standing rivalry.

"Oh, I'm not into sports that much," she answered, leaning back in her chair, looking all too innocent. "But I'll happily watch from the sidelines."

"Well, what?" Scott spoke up above their heads. "You know I never turn down a friendly game."

"You're on." Haley gave a thumbs-up and jumped to her feet, leaving her plate half-full.

"Oh, must we?" came a female voice from another table. "I'd enjoy a nice quiet game of bridge, myself."

From the sleepy droop of Ivy's lids and the smudges under her eyes, Noah wasn't too sure she wouldn't fall asleep over a subdued bridge game. He knew she'd put in a long week at the store, and Aunt Arletta had let it slip that her niece had been late home the night before, out having a social hour with a client. That he'd discovered the client was Gerry Reeves nettled him more than he'd like to admit, even to himself.

"Bridge is boring," Scott argued. "C'mon, Val. You can't have your pick of things to do every time."

"But I hate basketball!" Val whined. "I'm no good at it."

"Doesn't matter," Scott said with determination. "Kelly plays, and she's not much good at it, either."

Kelly punched her husband in playful protest. Scott laughingly grabbed her fist and held tight, shooting her a tender grin. "We'll team up so that everyone gets a turn," he added.

Noah turned his raised-brow stare directly at Ivy. "Great idea, pal," he agreed. "Everybody plays. No slackers."

"There's too many people for everybody to play," Ivy argued.

"Hmm, you're right, I guess. Okay. But you play, too, or I don't."

Haley groaned. "Please, Ivy. Say you'll play. I want a chance, just one, to beat Scotty at the game, or his head will be the size of a basketball again and I'll have to listen to his bragging all week. And I can't do it all by myself. I have a feeling I need Noah to be on my team."

Ivy looked doubtful. "I'm not fast enough for it."

"You don't have to stay in long," Haley insisted. "Does she, Noah?"

"Ten minutes, then we'll let you off the hook."

"All right. But don't say I didn't warn you."

Haley pushed and hurried dinner along. "Save dessert," she begged. "I've a real player on my team now."

Good-naturedly, the crowd complied, cleaning up the food tables and folding them away with more speed than usual while Haley gathered a hand-picked few into a huddle. Noah played starting guard, Ivy forward. The game began among friendly challenges from both sides, swiftly proceeding to hoots and cheers.

A few minutes into the game, Ivy caught the ball on rebound, stepping sideways as she dribbled. An opposing player began to crowd her. Noah was somewhere close by, but she didn't take time to look. The next thing she knew, her shoulder slammed into his hard body and they stumbled, tripping over each other. Automatically his hand circled her shoulders to stabilize her, but it was too late. They both went down.

"Time," Haley called.

Above them the play stopped. Ivy heard her own harshly pulled breath, her lungs heaving. For a long second she lay against Noah's arm, his near-to-normal breath showing his fitness. He said nothing. She felt as though she might sound like a bumbling idiot if she tried to speak while she gasped for air, so she settled for merely returning his stare.

Something very tender and protective lay near the surface of his gaze. She noticed a tiny half-moon scar near his right eye and had the wild impulse to touch it. In fact, her fingers nearly itched to touch his face.

She held herself in check, but just barely, and dropped her lashes. His mouth softened, parted as though he might kiss her.

Shock ran through her as she realized she'd welcome his lips on hers.

If a crowd hadn't been circling them, Ivy was sure he would have. Her heart raced harder.

"Are you hurt, Ivy?" Noah finally murmured.

She had to clear her throat before she could answer. "No."

He moved, then, leaping up and pulling her to stand.

"Are you okay?" Kelly, Scott, and the others looked anxious.

"I'm fine, really," she quickly reassured, responding to Noah's tug and then heading for the sidelines. "Just had the wind knocked out of me."

In more ways than one. Her heart continued to race, but she suspected it wasn't from the active game.

"You're sure?" Scott asked, practically hovering. "We could have Donna look you over."

"Donna?" Noah asked.

"Donna's a nurse," Ivy explained to Noah before turning to Scotty. "I appreciate the thought, but I don't need her."

"Sure?" Noah insistently queried. Ball tucked under his arm, he walked backward, watching her face. He hadn't even worked up a sweat, she noticed.

"Just winded. Haley, I've had my ten minutes. Put another player in."

"All right. You take it easy, now. C'mon, Noah."

With a last glance, Noah followed Haley to the center of the court while Ivy sank gratefully to the floor and rested her back against the wall. Her chin stung where she'd scraped the floor; she'd have a nice scab by tomorrow. Kelly brought her a cool damp cloth and Ivy used it to wipe her face, and a cup of water. She'd been put together with all the coordination of a string puppet, she guessed as she sipped. Besides that, she'd never had much time in her youth to play games.

Except for the growing-up kind.

Eric had played sports. Everything—football, basketball, baseball, track. At sixteen, she'd been captivated by Eric and he by her. They even planned to elope until discovered by his parents, who threatened to take away all of his sports if Eric didn't break up with her. They hadn't approved of her at all.

Eric had chosen his sports and his parents' edict. He stumbled through a breakup speech, leaving her brokenhearted. Yet Ivy understood his need to obey his parents, and placed her hopes in time. Time for his parents to get to know her, to eventually accept her. Before that could happen, within weeks, she saw Eric walking the school halls hand in hand with a new girlfriend. He walked right by her without speaking.

It hurt like a sharp blade slicing into her right arm. It was Kelly and Aunt Arletta who stood staunchly beside her until she stopped crying. Later, she'd stuffed the simple white dress she'd chosen to be married in during those delirious, hazy days of teenage dreams into the farthest corner of her closet. That spring she'd taken a second job with the largest department store in the city.

And she'd stopped playing games. They only took up one's time, she reasoned with Kelly, and she'd had no more time for such childish endeavors.

Obviously, Noah had. A lot of time. Ivy watched his graceful, adroit movements and thought him a beautiful animal in motion. No one gained that kind of skill without a great deal of time invested in the practice of it.

Lord, have mercy on me, she silently prayed. *He's just altogether too attractive for his own good. Or mine. Lord, You know I can't afford to fall in love with someone like him. He has so little ambition beyond being a gardener....*

Adam was a gardener, a gentle reminder came. *And My son a carpenter.*

All true, Ivy thought. But she lived in a more complicated world, and she wanted a better existence than one provided by a mere gardener. She wanted a big enough bank account to never feel the rough edges of near poverty ever again. Being poor scared her. Sometimes, although she kept her fears secret even from Aunt Arletta, she had awful moments when she thought she'd never make her monthly obligations. That her store might fail.

Sighing, she put the thought away. Those were fears she confessed only to the Lord, and then only in the quiet of night. This was a good season, her year hadn't been a bad one at all. She had no reason to worry.

Noah made a last basket with grace, and their impromptu umpire called the game. Haley and her teammates swarmed around Noah with high-spirited compliments before Haley marched over to Scotty in high glee over their win.

The group ate dessert and coffee quickly, with loads of post-game banter. Then most began to head home.

"See you Sunday," Kelly said as she hugged Ivy good-night.

"Good game, Noah," Scott added with good nature. "I'll take a rematch anytime. Glad to have you around, buddy."

Ivy said little on their drive home until they were nearly there. "Now that you feel at home with the singles at church, you can find a game whenever you want it," she remarked casually. "There's usually someone ready to play."

"Yeah, probably true." Stopped for a red light, he glanced at her. "But there's other things I like to do besides play basketball."

"Well, you sure made a hit with Haley and Scott."

"Mmm. Now tell me again, how did you know I like the game?"

"You need ask?" she reminded him.

"That's right. Aunt Arletta," he recalled, chuckling. "That is one feisty lady. She asks so many questions she could qualify for the CIA, FBI and the local psychiatry board all at the same time."

"Yep, that's Aunt A, all right. She'd dig out the mysteries of the sphinx, if she could get it to talk. You're lucky she hasn't told you what to wear yet," Ivy muttered as they pulled into the apartment parking lot.

"Oh, she did. Told me to wear jeans and sneakers

tonight, but I might need a new cardigan sweater for casual Sundays. She doesn't like the old gray one I've been wearing."

Ivy groaned and leaned her head against the back rest. "That's not too bad. Have you met Bill Warner yet? The music director? She once told Bill to stop wearing white shirts because they made his skin look pasty. And Kelly designs her own clothes, so you can imagine what she sometimes has to say when Kelly shows up in a new outfit. And one time, she told a complete stranger, a car salesman, that he should buy a better toupee or not wear one at all."

Chuckling, Noah glanced at the light showing from Ivy's apartment window. "Well, it looks as though she's waiting up." He opened his door and got out. "C'mon, I'll walk you to your door."

Ivy took three steps toward the walk, then stopped abruptly. Her car wasn't in her space. Another occupied it. Slowly, she turned, looking down the line of filled spaces. Her car wasn't there.

"What's the matter, Ivy?"

"My car is gone."

"Are you sure? Perhaps you've forgotten where you parked."

"Yes, I'm very sure. I parked there, under the streetlight when I came home from the store. It was there when you picked me up."

"Perhaps your aunt drove it."

"She doesn't drive, but she did once—" Turning, Ivy raced up the walk and skidded to a stop in front of her first-floor apartment. She fumbled with her keys. Calmly, Noah took them from her hand.

"Aunt Arletta," she called even before the door was completely opened. Arletta lay curled against one corner of the blue-plaid sofa, hot-pink fuzzy slippers on her feet. Shirley occupied the other end, watching TV.

"Hello, dear. Did you two have a nice time?"

"Aunt Arletta, my car's not in its usual spot." Ivy swallowed, trying to keep the panic from exploding. "Do you know anything about that?"

"Oh, yes, actually, I do," Arletta said, smoothing her fire-engine-red robe over her ankles. Her hair was done up in old-fashioned pin curls. "Shirley's daughter needed to borrow it for a little while."

"A little while? How long do you mean?"

"Only overnight, dear. She'll be back tomorrow afternoon sometime. That is, if her mother-in-law isn't any worse."

Shirley's eyes grew apprehensive. "I hope you don't object, Ivy. Candy's car wouldn't start and she needed to drive Jason and David to Springfield to see their other grandmother. The dear soul is in the hospital, you see, and desperately wanted to see the boys."

"Uh, but...Aunt Arletta..."

Ivy wanted to ask where the boys' father was, but she was afraid she knew the answer to that one. David Sr., Shirley's son-in-law, usually spent his time with his drinking buddies. It left Candy to take the lion's share of raising their boys and supporting the household, and Shirley worried herself sick over them all. Ivy daren't ask why David hadn't taken responsibility for driving his family down to see his mother without causing Shirley to gush into tears.

Glancing from one to the other lined face, Ivy felt like an ungracious wretch. How could she reprove her aunt's generosity when the need was so great?

But the last time Aunt Arletta had loaned Ivy's car to someone it had come back empty of gas and with a new dent in the back fender.

The trouble was, Aunt Arletta didn't think about those things. She only saw a need to be filled.

"Uh, it's all right, Shirley. I—" She drew a deep breath and tried to appear unconcerned as she unbuttoned her jacket and slid it from her shoulders. "We'll just walk to church in the morning. I'm sure Candy will be back by tomorrow night."

She could only hope Candy would remember she needed the car on Monday. She couldn't get along without her own transportation for long.

"Oh." Shirley's mouth began to quiver. "It has made a hardship for you."

"No, no. I'm sorry, Shirley. We'll find a ride, don't worry."

"No need for that, ladies," Noah spoke up. "I'll run you all to church."

"In your truck, no doubt," Ivy said under her breath. She bit her underlip at the edge of irritation she'd let show.

"What's wrong with my truck?"

"Nothing," she let her quarrelsome tone die. It wasn't a huge problem; she was just too tired to think properly. She hated to depend on someone else for transportation; it made her feel too helpless. "Only, it's a little cold to be riding in the open truck bed. There's only room for two in front."

"That's easily solved, Ivy." He shoved his hands into his back pockets. "I'll make two runs. The five-mile round trip will be a snap, considering you mentioned walking as an alternative."

"We've walked it before," she said.

"Uh-huh. It might be all in a morning for you, but it seems going a little far to ask these two ladies to hike that on a cold Sunday morning."

"Now see here, Noah," Aunt Arletta said, her mouth in a pout as she stood up. "I can still hobble along without breaking a leg."

"Walking is good exercise," Ivy insisted, lifting her chin, but then admitted, "I don't suppose I really meant us all to walk the whole five miles. We can call for the church bus to make a stop for us." For some reason she felt annoyed with Noah; she didn't want him solving her problems for her. She wanted to solve them herself, her own way.

"Children, really—" Aunt Arletta began.

"Uh-huh. Don't think the church bus runs its route this way, either," he answered with a look that clearly said she was making a mountain from a tiny ant mound.

"We gladly accept your offer, Noah," Aunt Arletta said without further ado. "Don't we, Shirley?"

"Oh, my. Yes. Yes, indeed, if you're sure..."

"Well, we might just have called a cab," Ivy muttered.

"Uh-huh," he said again, altogether too satisfied. A little too smugly, for Ivy's peace of mind. "But now there's no need."

Oh, fine! Another male who wanted the last word in any discussion.

Chapter Six

Ivy checked over the weekly receipts one more time, her best of any since she'd opened the store. Sherri was right; there had been a significant increase in their business lately, and she'd had several new referrals from both Gerald and Barbara Reeves.

Imagine that. She didn't know why the brother and sister had decided to take her under their wing, but she was grateful. At this rate she'd have to increase Emily's and Brad's hours or add another holiday clerk.

She glanced at her watch. Eight o'clock. She had to be downtown at nine-thirty.

Her referral this morning had come from Noah, of all people. A small law firm wanted a professional decorator for Christmas, and specifically requested a Nativity theme. Noah planned on providing the live trees, but had called on her to create the rest of it. Seasonal decorating as a service was a little out of her line, but she looked forward to the challenge.

A knock on the front door caused her to rise from

her stool in the back room where she worked at her tiny desk. Too early to open, Ivy hoped it might be Emily.

It was Gerry. She hadn't heard from him since the night they'd had dessert and coffee. She thought he'd had a good time, then wondered if she'd put him off from calling her again by being too talkative, or acting too available.

"Hi," he offered with a quick smile. "Tried to call your home, but you'd gone already. Do you always come in with the dawn?"

"'Hard work brings a profit,'" Noah said as he came up carrying a cardboard tray holding two foam coffee cups and a couple of wrapped breakfast sandwiches. "'But mere talk leads only to poverty.'"

A brief look of annoyance shot across Gerry's handsome features before he schooled his expression into blandness. "Another one of your Proverbs, Noah?"

"Yep." Noah's eyes were unrepentant. "Proverbs 14, verse 23. Best motivational messages ever written."

"So you've said," Gerry muttered ironically. "On a number of occasions. What are you doing here, Noah?"

"I have a delivery to make." Noah returned the other man's challenge with "What are you doing here?"

Gerry's chin hardened. "I've come to make an appointment with Ivy, if you don't mind."

"Business or personal?"

"I really don't see that it concerns you one way or another, Noah."

"That's your trouble, Gerry. You don't see a lot of things."

"Well, come in, both of you," Ivy insisted, hoping her business tone would dampen the smoldering undercurrent between these two. "You're letting in the cold air."

She snapped on the front overhead lights and led the way back to her register counter. She pulled out the key to the back door.

"What do you have, Noah?"

"Matthew and I came up with a couple of wooden stables that'll be great for a floor nativity. Think you'll like 'em. Matt's pretty good with angels, too. Brought one along with breakfast."

"That's very sweet of you. Why don't you set breakfast down on the back desk and unload the merchandise you brought. I'll be with you in a moment."

"Okay." But he made no immediate move to leave.

Ignoring him, Ivy turned to Gerry. "What is it you wanted to see me about?"

Gerry eyed Noah with an expectant go-away gaze. When Noah still made no move toward attending his own business, Gerry attempted to glaze his annoyance with amusement. It didn't quite cover it, though, and Ivy caught edges of his growing anger.

If she didn't do something quickly, she might have a real altercation going. She offered Gerry her most encouraging smile.

"I have a project I want to discuss with you, Ivy," Gerry finally said.

Noah gave a smothered "hmmph," but when Ivy tossed him a seriously determined glare over her shoulder, he finally turned on his heel and disappeared beyond the back room door.

"Certainly," Ivy answered Gerry calmly in her professional voice. "Later this week all right? How about Friday?"

The grating back door sound carried through, then boots slapping the cement. Gerry peered past the half-opened door to make sure he and Ivy could not be overheard before he relaxed with a widening smile.

"That'll do, I suppose." He brushed his fingers through his moonlight swag of hair, straightened a perfectly straight red silk tie, and lowered his voice. "But I really came to invite you to dinner Wednesday evening. Barbara and I are entertaining a couple from Chicago at Chase's on the Plaza, and we'd love to have you join us."

The Plaza was an upscale shopping neighborhood that drew visitors nationwide at any time, but especially during the weeks before Christmas. Ivy only wished she had enough money to expand and take a second store into the exclusive area.

"Wednesday..." Feeling enormously flattered, Ivy considered the invitation. Dinner at Chase's tempted her mightily. She'd never had a meal there; her budget didn't stretch that far.

"Oh, Gerry, I wish I could..." she began, taking a deep breath. "But during the Christmas season the store remains open until eight, and I usually pick up Aunt Arletta from midweek prayer service straight afterward."

"Oh. Well, couldn't you find someone to close for you? And I can send a cab for your aunt. Please say you'll come, Ivy," he coaxed. His eyelids drooped in further invitation. "Barbara already has a dinner partner for the evening, and we won't be seated until about seven-thirty."

"Well in that case, I'd love to come," she replied quickly, unable to resist the prospect of such an evening. Her mind leapt toward asking Sherri to stay the extra hours, and what she should wear.

"Good. I'll send a car for you."

"That's sweet of you, Gerry, but why don't I meet you there? Then you'll be free to entertain your guests without worrying about me. Besides, I prefer to drive so I can go straight home at the close of the evening. Sorry, but I can't keep late hours during the week."

He looked a little disappointed and as if he wanted to argue his case, but then relented. "All right. If you insist. I suppose that would be best."

Gerry said goodbye and left, and Ivy turned to see what might be keeping Noah only to discover nothing was. He stood just inside the back room, hands tucked into his back pockets, his eyes narrowed in thoughtful contemplation.

"Oh!" She halted. "I didn't hear you come back in."

"You weren't listening." He began to stack her papers to clear a place for the coffee. "Sit. Eat your breakfast."

She checked her watch again. "I have to leave in ten minutes for the law office where you recommended me. What makes you think I want anything to eat?"

"Aunt Arletta said you left home before six this morning."

"Are you and Aunt A into a conspiracy or something?"

"Protein in the morning stays with you."

He pulled up an old crate and sat to unwrap his own sandwich. "Nearly cold," he grumbled. "Got a microwave?"

"Well, I hardly knew you were coming, did I?" She gave him a reproving glance. "And I don't have room for a microwave in here."

"Thought I'd catch you before your doors opened."

"I have to take care of business when I can, early or late. You should know that. How is it for you in the spring and summer? I'll bet you don't turn down a sale during your busiest season," she said, ignoring the fact that Gerry's visit had really been personal. Why should she account to Noah about whom she dated?

He grunted and chewed. "Crazy. Barely enough time to breathe. Want to come out to see the tree farm on Sunday afternoon?"

"Sunday?" His startling change of directions left her a little breathless. She wasn't sure if his "crazy" was directed at her growing association with Gerry or that seasonal business was often crazy.

"Aunt Arletta said she'd love to see my place. 'Course it's kinda bare right now. This is my resting season."

"You don't deal with Christmas items, then?"

"Nope. Oh, I have a few business accounts that I provide trees and greenery for. Like the one I suggested your services to, but I decided long ago to enjoy December without working myself into a state of whether I could make the holidays pay off or not." He shook his head. "Christmas trees are chancy."

"What about these things you brought today?"

"That's mostly Matt's doing and I don't have to put in too much time when they're sold in a shop like yours."

A knock came from the front glass. "That'll be Sherri or Emily," she said, sipping the last of her coffee. She rose to open the front door.

"How about Sunday?" he called after her.

"All right," she returned over her shoulder. The outing sounded like one that would appeal to Aunt Arletta. She loved the parks and they seldom had a chance to visit the countryside, especially in winter. "If you're sure you want to take us both around, we'd love to come."

After she'd let Sherri in, she returned to the back room. Noah'd tossed her back door key on her desk and left.

Toward noon, she returned to Wall's Intrigue, very pleased with her morning. The law firm liked her suggestions and gave her a substantial amount to cover the order; her mind played with all the possibilities.

It wasn't until a lull in store traffic that evening that she explored the box Noah had brought. She examined the small wood stables, embossed with moss and wood shavings. They had a rough charm and Ivy knew instinctively which customers would find the miniature stables appealing. They were perfect for housing the tiny nativity figures.

From the last corner of the box, she uncovered a piece of polished wood with a face carved into one side. Ivy couldn't tell if it was intended to be a male or female. A much finer piece than the others Noah had brought, the face had a tender quality, a lively look of expectation and joy. Behind the head, wings swept upward and disappeared into the curved wood.

A prickling crawled up the back of her neck. Running a fingertip along the features, she could almost envision the live model, a reality of breathtaking beauty.

Aunt Arletta believed in the presence of angels, and although she'd admitted she'd never seen one, Aunt A insisted her friend Shirley had. Ivy believed the Scriptures about the heavenly beings, too, but had seldom given them much thought. With the recent resurgence in popularity of their portrayal as art objects and the beauty of this piece, she thought the carving would command a healthy price if shown in a more prestigious gallery.

Who had carved it? Ivy knew many local artists, but she'd never seen this artist's work. Noah had said it came from his friend Matt.

The phone rang, interrupting her thoughts. She set the piece aside, determining to get an appraisal from an associate. And she planned on questioning Noah further as to its origin.

At the close of the Sunday morning service, Ivy and Aunt Arletta piled into Noah's truck for the drive out to his nursery farm. Directing Ivy to scoot across the bench seat first, he lent a strong arm for the older woman and provided a couple of small pillows for her comfort.

"Put a beef stew in the slow cooker before I left this morning," he said as he tucked Arletta's skirt out of the door's way. "Should be good and tender by the time we get there. Then we'll be fortified for the big walk."

"How much land do you have?" Ivy asked.

"About twenty-five acres. Not as much as I'd like, but all I can take care of for a while yet. Don't want to expand until—" Noah suddenly clipped his thought with a tightening of his mouth.

Ivy tried to read his expression, wondering what bitter thought had run through his head. It seemed so unlike Noah to harbor so negative an emotion, it surprised her. But his profile told her nothing, and he showed her even less of it as he pointed out a huge bird sitting atop a telephone pole as they left the city behind. "There's a red-tailed hawk."

"Oh, so it is," Aunt Arletta replied with awed enjoyment. "There's another. We don't get to see them in the city."

"No, they like to hunt open fields," he replied, and launched into a discussion of the bird population that lived nearby.

South of the outlying suburbs they left the main highway, traveling a few miles on a secondary road before turning into a gravel drive. A huge barn and storage shed shared an L-shaped configuration with two old aluminum-sided trailers. An extended redwood deck and walkway connected the two, but they were each identified with signs as office and private.

Beyond, a field of early growth hardwood trees appeared stark against the gray November sky. A gathering heaviness filled the air with moisture, giving the hint they could receive an early snow.

"Welcome, ladies," Noah said, the light of pride showing in his glance.

A huge ginger cat came out from beneath the deck

to greet them. One ear was mutilated and he had a long scar on one cheek, but his fur was shiny and fluffed. He mewed loudly and twined himself against Ivy's legs.

"Well, hello, there, old fellow." She bent to run a finger against his ear.

"That's Sampson," Noah said.

"Looks like he's well named," Aunt Arletta remarked. "He must help keep the mice population in check."

"Yeah, he does all right," Noah replied as he unlocked the smaller of the two trailers. "I'm surprised he's taken to you, Ivy. He mostly makes himself scarce when other people are around. He comes in with me only when he's looking for a little warmth."

"It appears he's hungry this time," Aunt Arletta said.

"Seems so." Noah watched as Ivy continued to stroke the cat. When she began to withdraw, Sampson rubbed his cheek against her hand, begging for more. Noah had a distinct feeling of envy at her immediate response of loving treatment.

"Come inside," he said, letting out his breath, "and we'll find him something and have a bite to eat ourselves before I show you over the place. But I've been here in the Midwest for only two years and haven't had time to build everything I want to yet."

Inside, he turned on the heat. "We'll be toasty in a few minutes. Wish it had been a nicer day to show you the fields. You don't really see much happening with trees in winter. But in spring and autumn... Anyway, take a seat."

"Ivy, you can change into your jeans and boots back there—" he nodded toward the tiny bedroom in the back "—while I feed Sampson and set the table."

Ivy followed his direction, laying her rolled jeans and heavy sweatshirt on the bed as she shed her black wool skirt and cream-colored silk blouse. She wondered how he moved around in the miniature room; the full-size bed took the entire space. It was neatly made without a spread, blankets neatly folded down to show flannel sheets beneath. Pegs on the opposite wall held clothes. A long shelf ran the length of the room above the bed, full to overflowing with books, mostly concerned with his business, and a few pictures.

She noticed one with Noah in cap and gown between an older couple. His parents, probably, she speculated.

A wind blast rocked the trailer, sending chills through her. The structure wasn't any too warm, she shiveringly noted, and wondered if Noah minded the cold.

As she hurriedly reached for her jeans, she discovered a spot on the blanket where ginger-colored hair clung. Sampson lay there more often than Noah was willing to admit, she guessed. Maybe they both sought a little warmth and comfort.

"Now, you're my guests today, Aunt A," Noah said as Ivy rejoined the two in the living room. He placed a bowl of stew and a paper towel on the fold-out table in front of her aunt and another on the permanent table just big enough for two.

Outside, the wind picked up again, giving teeth to the promise of an early winter. "You know, I believe it's spitting a little rain outside," Aunt Arletta remarked with a doubtful air. "Perhaps we should postpone our tour."

Noah glanced out the window, and slowly nodded. "If you think that's best, Aunt A."

Ivy took a quick peek at Noah, then declared, "I'm still game, for a little while, at least. But you don't have to come, Aunt Arletta. You can wait in here out of the weather."

"Of course," Noah agreed quickly as another gust hit the trailer. "You just sit tight and enjoy your tea."

"Well, I'd still love seeing everything. If you don't go too fast or too far..."

"I'll tell you what. I've got an old golf cart out in the barn, Aunt A. Let me go get it and we can tuck you up with a blanket."

"That'll do," she said, nodding her agreement.

They finished their meal quickly, and true to his promise, Noah made the cart comfortable. With mittened hands, Ivy drove it slowly down the farm track while Noah walked or trotted beside them, making occasional stops to discuss what he'd planted, growth patterns and species, and his plans for as yet unplanted fields. Sampson accompanied them, sometimes roaming ahead to search out an interesting clump of dirt.

"I'm still small, but I'm growing. We offer garden design and implementation on a staggered basis, according to a home owner's budget. We're in a co-op with half a dozen growers who specialize in shrubs and flowers. I designed and put in a water lily garden last summer at one referral," he said, eyes sparkling.

Noah glanced their way frequently, the wind whipping his hair about, some of it into his eyes. Without pausing, he took a knit hat from his heavy jacket and pulled it over his head and ears, giving him the appearance of an overgrown boy. Ivy felt her heart skid and bump—a little too uncomfortably for her own peace of mind—and instantly reined in her emotions. Noah was still a mere gardener.

"We want to do more of that kind of thing, but weekly lawn care provides our bread and butter. But I want to carry garden decorations, pots of flowers and herbs for the deck, houseplants and benches. I hope to eventually keep my men on the payroll full-time, too, even through the winter. We don't get enough call for snow removal, but I don't want to get into Christmas decorations. Too many people already do that."

Aunt Arletta nodded as though she understood or agreed to everything Noah said.

"That's wise of you, Noah. Don't you think so, Ivy? Knowing where to emphasize your strengths is a great asset. Now, if you ask me, you should concentrate on more showy plants near the entrance to this place—" Arletta waved an arm freely to make her point as they made their way back "—and around this office. Give people something to look at they'll want for themselves."

"Aunt Arletta, I think Noah can make his own plans without help from us." Ivy halted the golf cart besides the wooden walk.

"Oh, but dear, he needs a little feminine viewpoint, to my way of thinking. To reach his potential, don't you see."

"Um..." Ivy glanced apologetically toward Noah, but he didn't seem overly offended by her aunt's opinions. On the contrary, his eyes sparkled with laughter while his mouth curved into a knowing grin as he offered an arm to help her aunt from the cart. A very knowing grin.

Ivy didn't quite know what to do with the wayward feeling that traveled all the way to her toes with that smile. Or trust it, either. But she wasn't going to give in to it.

Chapter Seven

Chase's turned out to be everything Ivy had read, heard, or dreamed of in a fine restaurant. Subdued lighting. Crisp linens and fine china. Tasteful decor, a soft piano, and finally, old-world-polite waiters who served with unobtrusive precision.

Barbara and her date talked racketball while the visiting Chicago couple, the Sanders, spoke of a recent trip to the French countryside to look for antiques. An attentive Gerry made Ivy feel as if she'd stepped into Cinderella's shoes.

"Say, Gerry—" William leaned forward slightly "—we ran into the Thorntons a couple of weeks ago. Don't see them much anymore, but we served on the same hospital board for a long time. He mentioned his boy, Noah, is located somewhere around here. Didn't you two belong to the same circles at college?"

William Sanders knew Noah's parents? Ivy glanced between the men, her curiosity instantly piqued. Neither Gerry nor Noah behaved as friends.

They acted more like old adversaries rather than college buddies. Did their association hold more than a simple business connection?

There had been that odd, almost intimate scene between Barbara and Noah in her shop that first day—which had made her wonder...

All at once she thought herself completely dense. Why hadn't she paid better attention? Noah and Barbara?

The idea made her want to sit up straight and perk her ears. Or lean forward to somehow entice forth a little more information, though Ivy couldn't imagine why. She reminded herself that she'd chosen not to have a romantic interest in Noah. It just wouldn't work. He didn't want the same things in life she wanted.

She jerked her focus back to Gerry's face, the self-conscious, indolent way he leaned easily against the high wing back chair he occupied. He used his body to display grace in movement or repose, like a still life painting or an old movie, while Noah always seemed animated, full of thought, and totally unaware of the beauty of his athletic body. Noah and Gerry were so different, she couldn't think of what they might have had in common even in the beginning.

"So we did," Gerry answered with a wry curve to his lips. He glanced at Ivy and gave an enigmatic shrug. "Yes, Noah's about the area somewhere. He's busy doing...whatever it is he does."

"Oh, Nancy," Barbara interrupted "you must try to get by Ivy's shop before you fly home. She has the cutest little interior design store, and her art wall features some offbeat talent you may like."

"That's kind of you to recommend Wall's Intrigue, Barbara," Ivy said, reluctant to change the subject. She'd hoped to hear more of Gerry's connection with Noah. "But Nancy, I haven't any antiques and my merchandise appeals mostly to a modest budget."

"Don't be so humble, Ivy." Gerry insisted. "You have a wonderful eye for the artists you display."

"Thank you, Gerry. Actually, an unusual piece came in quite recently, a piece of wood sculpture from, um, from an artist unknown to me. I think it may be worth quite a nice sum."

"What is so unusual about it?" Nancy asked.

"Oh, it's...it's a face." Ivy searched for words to explain the feeling the sculpture gave her. "A remarkable representation of an angel. Something about it seems so joyous, it speaks."

"You do make it sound intriguing, Ivy," Barbara mused. "Perhaps I'll pop in tomorrow myself to see it."

The conversation languished for another twenty minutes before Ivy thanked Gerry for dinner, said polite good-nights, and excused herself. Gerry walked her to her car.

"Thank you for coming, Ivy." He leaned against the open door, loath to let her go so soon. "You're a charming dinner companion. How about coming to lunch on Friday? I could use your advice. I have to meet with a committee from a woman's shelter to plan a fund-raiser."

"You want my advice for a fund-raiser?"

"Sure. You're a fresh voice."

"But Gerry, I've had no experience with fund-raising."

"You have a good business head, Ivy. And your creativity is priceless. Please say you'll come. I'd like to see you more, but—" he grimaced, letting her understand his objections "—you seem to work all the time. This way I can claim your time where you can give it without feeling guilty. Besides, I need you on my side. Barbara wants to do another dinner dance, but overdone charity dances are boring. I think people are tired of those."

She had to admit it. The flattery went right to her head. He thought her creative and capable. Was this finally the right man for her? He had everything on her list of most desirable traits for possible husband candidates, except…

Except an image of Noah's sparkling eyes swam into her consciousness, effectively blotting out Gerry's handsome features.

"I'd be delighted to come, Gerry," she replied swiftly, pushing the image aside. "Tell me when and where to meet you."

Aunt Arletta was sound asleep when she let herself into the apartment. Ivy tiptoed into her aunt's bedroom, slipped the open Bible from her hands, and removed her glasses. Ivy examined the soft, pink face, the multitude of lines giving character to Arletta's features. When she was a little girl, Ivy thought they stood for love lines and tried to count them. She'd asked her dad why she couldn't have some, too. He'd replied that she'd have them in plenty one day when she'd lived long enough to earn them.

The thought of never earning them fretted her a little; her dad had died before he could collect his.

She glanced down at the scripture Arletta had been

reading. "'Let not your heart be troubled...'" John, another of Aunt A's Biblical favorites.

Ivy wished she felt as comfortable trusting in all the old promises as her aunt did. She wanted to trust in them, but life was sometimes such a struggle to balance all its parts. Perhaps it would take those lines in her own face before she achieved that balance.

Setting aside the Bible, she turned off the light and tiptoed from the room. Moments later, she punched in Kelly's number from the phone in her own room.

"Hi, Kelly. I found a note from Aunt A that says you called." She kicked off her shoes and lay back. "What's up?"

"Haven't seen you much lately, Ivy, except for quick passes at church. I'm lonesome for a good old-fashioned girl's chat. What about you and Noah coming to dinner Saturday night after the store closes?"

"Noah and me?"

"What's that hesitation I hear?"

"Um..."

"C'mon, give. Looked to me like you and Noah were developing quite nicely into a couple during that basketball game the other night."

"Kelly, Noah and I are not a couple."

"You could have fooled me," Kelly replied, teasing.

"You can just rethink that one. For your information, Aunt Arletta arranged it." She almost gave a sniff as she struggled not to sound like a queen-size snob. "Noah is only someone I do business with."

"Uh-huh..."

That was the trouble with close friends. They knew you too well. She took a deep breath, insisting,

"Honestly, Kelly, we're just friends. Or rather, he's a friend of Aunt Arletta's."

"You're kidding!"

"Not a bit."

Kelly chuckled. "What's Aunt Arletta got on him?"

"Nothing." Ivy blinked, letting her laughter show in her voice. "They seem to genuinely like each other."

"Well, that's a first. She's never liked any of the others. Well, neither did I, after all was over. But Scott really likes Noah and I want a closer look at him, too. Must be something to Aunt A's instincts sometimes. Why don't you like him?"

"I didn't say I dislike him. I don't dislike him at all. I...he's, um, it's..." Taking a deep breath, she plunged ahead. "I'm just interested in someone else."

"Oh? Who?" came the interested challenge.

Ivy's breath left her in a sigh of relief for successfully sidetracking her too astute friend. "Gerry Reeves. You know, he and his sister, Barbara, own Reeves House, where you were married? They're all over the social scene when it comes to charities and prominent city affairs."

"You're kidding! That Gerald Reeves? What's he like?"

"Oh, Kelly—" she rolled over to her stomach "—he matches everything I have on my list for a desirable husband. He's from a well-established family—"

"You mean wealthy?"

"Well, yes, he is. And, Kelly, he runs in the greatest circles."

"Hmm....what's he do?"

"Well, he takes care of family investments and involves himself in a lot of philanthropic projects and charity organizations."

"Is that all? Doesn't he have a profession?"

"Why, I really haven't asked." She cradled her cheek. "I think it's just enough to look after the estate and family fortune. Kelly, he has invited me to help him organize a fund-raising event for a new woman's shelter. Deborah's Dwelling, named for his grandmother."

"Are you going to do it?"

"Yes, sure. Why shouldn't I? I'm already seeing a lot more traffic in the store because of Gerry and Barbara. This is a chance to not only work for a worthy cause, but as Gerry pointed out, it's good for business, too."

A long pause followed before Kelly replied. "No reason, I guess. If you want to, go for it. But how about Saturday? We're going out of town to Scott's parents for Thanksgiving. It's the last time I'll get a chance to see you 'til almost Christmas."

"Oh, all right. But tell Scott what I said. Noah and I are not a couple. Only friends."

Only friends...only friends... Ivy kept the phrase at a near chant as Scott chatted of "you and Ivy" once more over dessert, mentioning a young couples' Christmas dinner being planned at church. He'd used the term half a dozen times during dinner.

Ivy shot a pleading gaze toward Kelly.

"Let's take our coffee into the living room," Kelly hastily suggested, rising from the table. "Hon, why don't you pull out the snapshots of those two houses we looked at the other day?''

Kelly led the way to the couch, inviting Ivy to share it, while Scott rummaged in the small rolltop desk against the wall. Noah took the overstuffed chair by the window.

Ivy sat against the couch corner, folding her legs beneath her.

''The one I like best needs a lot of work,'' Scott mumbled, shuffling through several snapshots, ''but we can do most of it ourselves if we take it. Say, Noah, if you could give me an idea of what I'd need to do to get the yard in shape...''

''You're looking at houses?'' Ivy questioned, turning her gaze on Kelly. ''You've only been married a few weeks. I thought you planned to stay in this apartment at least a year.''

''Yeah, well...'' Kelly shot a fond glance toward her new husband. ''We've been talking, and we don't want to wait any longer.'' She lowered her voice while the men pored over the pictures. ''We don't want to wait any longer to start a family, either. I know, Ivy, I know,'' she added, her glance full of laughter when Ivy raised a disbelieving brow.

Kelly was so proud of the carefully planned time line she'd made for her life before the wedding, Ivy couldn't believe her ears. Kelly had insisted it was essential to happiness. They'd discussed their five- and ten-year plans on many occasions, thinking themselves very wise and progressive in having one; and if Ivy was honest with herself, they'd even been a little smug toward their friends who didn't. They'd both wanted big things out of life. Now Kelly was throwing all that aside?

"But Kelly..."

"I didn't think I'd want to so soon either, Ivy, but now I do." Kelly reached for the snaps Scott handed her and passed them to Ivy. "Something... everything changed when Scott and I married. And Scott and I dated for three years. We're ready to move forward. We won't be able to afford anything but a small house this way, but money can't buy the real treasures in life, you know."

Aunt Arletta sometimes said the same thing, Ivy mused. She glanced at the small ranch house in the picture, about thirty years old, she guessed, with an overgrown yard. Something to whip into shape, Scott had just said. She'd never lived in a house with a yard of her own, although owning a house was indeed in her ten-year plan.

Her ten-year plan was dragging for sure, but she refused to give it up. She'd have a house one day, but she wanted something substantial. She'd decorate it in soft shades and graceful furniture, with a few fine art pieces for the walls, and entertain with style....

Laying the snapshot aside, she hid her sigh. Well...someday.

She noticed Noah enthusiastically pointing to something in another snapshot as Scott looked over his shoulder. His quick communicative glances were full of purpose as he talked. He certainly seemed happy while pursuing his own dreams. But they matched none of hers. She dreamed on a much larger scope.

"If you're sure," Ivy said, smoothing her long wool skirt across her knees. Her doubt of her friend's decision showed, and she felt ungracious in not giving her wholehearted approval. She hated to see Kelly lowering her goals.

Kelly merely smiled. "I am. Now tell me what happened yesterday." At Ivy's questioning gaze, she reminded, "Your meeting with Gerald Reeves? Are you going to work on this new charity?"

"Yes, I am," Ivy answered, letting her excitement cover her embarrassment at going blank over the question. She was trying to ignore the two men, and didn't want to admit she liked observing Noah in his animated discussion. It came to her that he was always full of life even while listening. He took in every movement, every shift in thought pattern as Scott spoke.

Deliberately, she turned back to Kelly.

"There are seven people on the planning committee," she said, "but Gerry's heading it. We ran through a lot of ideas and decided on two initial events to launch it, a dinner dance and a high-priced treasure hunt. Both events should bring in a lot of money. Wall's Intrigue will be listed as one of the sponsors."

"Sounds like you're moving in very grand circles, sweetie, something you've always wanted." Kelly lowered her voice. "And this personal thing with Gerry?"

"Hmm..." Ivy responded with a low tone. "Well, right now we're happy taking things slowly." She shrugged and picked at the buttons down the front of her skirt. "We're going out for breakfast in the morning before church. He isn't rushing me. But he likes my suggestions for his charity work and Barbara likes my store. In January, we'll start redecorating Reeves House's third floor. It'll pay a nice commission, actually."

"But it will take a lot of your time, won't it, between the charity work and the Reeves House project? Who'll watch the store? What does your aunt have to say to all this?"

"Oh, I'll have to increase Sherri's hours. My new clerk, Emily, is working out quite well. I'm hoping she'll agree to stay on longer than the holiday season. And you know Aunt Arletta."

Ivy said good-night shortly afterward, confessing to Kelly as she donned her heavy jacket that she still had to make a bank deposit. Her purse felt very heavy.

"You're kidding!" Kelly muttered, closing the door she'd just opened. "You still have to make a bank run yet tonight?"

"You mean you're still carrying the day's receipts?" Noah asked. His frown let her know how foolish he thought her action.

"Well, I had a last-minute customer who kept me late, and by the time she left, I just, um, came on. I didn't want to ruin your dinner, Kelly."

"Yeah, but Ivy..."

"Don't worry, this kind of thing doesn't happen often," Ivy assured, tugging on her gloves. "But it's the nature of owning a business. It's quite all right, I just drop it in the night deposit and then I'm on my way home. And it's only—" she peeled back the edge of her leather glove to glance at her watch, finding it nearer eleven than she thought "—um, not even midnight."

"I'll take you," Noah said without preamble or room for debate.

"That isn't necessary," Ivy returned.

"Maybe not, but you aren't going alone."

"Well, I've been alone many nights while locking up and making the bank run. What about your truck?"

Noah bridged that objection with a quick "I'll follow you, then."

"Ivy, please let Noah either take you or follow," Kelly urged. "For my peace of mind as well as your own safety. Just think of the scold I'd be in from Aunt Arletta if she ever discovered I let you travel the night streets with a large deposit."

"Kelly, Aunt A is aware of my business needs. She knows all about bank deposits."

"I'll bet she's never thought of how often you have to make one after dark, though," Noah insisted. "Honest, now...has she?"

"Well...not really. She thinks I do all my banking business during the day. But honestly, she wouldn't worry."

"No, she'd simply wait up every night praying for all the angels in heaven to guard your every move until you were safely home," Kelly said on a giggle.

"All right." Ivy gave in. "I suppose you're right."

Fifteen minutes later, Noah followed her slowly as she nosed her car close to the bank island so she could drop the night deposit. Usually, she thought little of the need to conduct business after dark, merely doing what had to be done, but now she felt glad for the good lighting around her. And Noah's presence. Traffic was thin, giving the business street an almost eerie, deserted air.

She pulled away from the bank and waved at

Noah, thinking he'd turn at the major street he needed to get back home, but he didn't. He followed her all the way to her apartment building and parked beside her. He cut his motor at the same time she did.

"That wasn't necessary, Noah," she told him as she slid from her car. "I'm quite capable of seeing myself home."

"Yeah, so I noticed." He fell into step beside her as she walked to the outer door.

"Well, as gallant as you are, this is nice. But you don't have to walk me to the door, really."

"Might as well. We're going to the same place."

"What do you mean?"

"Aunt A suggested I sleep on your couch tonight."

"She did?"

"Uh-huh. She kindly thought it more sensible for me than driving all the way home tonight when I have to drive back in the morning for church."

And that, Ivy thought, was Aunt Arletta. But what was she to do in the morning when Gerry came to pick her up for breakfast and found Noah sleeping in her living room?

Chapter Eight

A lamp glowed on the end table, and clean sheets and a blanket were neatly stacked on the couch. One of Ivy's pillows topped it.

Ivy knew without looking that Aunt Arletta had sweet rolls rising in the refrigerator for an early-morning bake. She always baked them for breakfast when they had a guest.

"I'm not sure how comfortable this old couch sleeps," Ivy murmured, wondering how Noah's tall frame would fare with the couch length. "It's developing lumps, I think."

"How would you know?" His mouth twitched into a grin. "Do you ever have time to test it?"

"Not much," she agreed. "I often come in only to go straight to bed."

"You work too many hours."

"And I suppose you don't?" She didn't want another sermon. Aunt Arletta sometimes said the same thing. "That's the price one pays for self-employment."

"You're right, it's a consuming enterprise to run a small business," he mused aloud. "Balance is the key. You should take more personal time."

"Maybe someday I will. But building my business is my first priority right now. Don't tell me you don't do the same thing when your season is in full swing. I hate to think of the kind of hours you put in then."

"But I don't take on more than I can handle."

"What are you talking about?"

"I—sorry, Ivy. I overheard you mentioning to Kelly about working with Gerald Reeves on a charity project. Are you sure you want to do that?"

"Why shouldn't I?"

"I know how demanding those committee jobs can become." He ran his hand against his temple, as though he picked up on her tiredness. "You're already putting in—what, about sixty to seventy hours a week? And this is your busiest time."

"Oh. Well—" she checked the bed clothing on the sofa "—my involvement is only for a few months and it's a wonderful cause. In fact, the committee could use another warm body with organizational skills and willing hands." Plumping the pillow, she glanced over her shoulder. "Why don't you join us?"

"I don't think so."

"The Old Garden Gate could win friends by being a sponsor."

"Not for me."

"Oh?" Surprised, she looked at him squarely. "I thought you were full of charity and generosity."

"I prefer to do other things with my extra time." His hands were stuck in his back pockets, a stance she was beginning to recognize as one of defense or deep thought. Why would he feel that way now, she wondered?

"Really, Noah, this is a great cause."

"I'm sure you're right. But I can't do the cause any good."

"You mean you don't want to be involved."

"That's right." His brown eyes became shuttered. "I haven't any more time for that sort of thing."

"But another woman's shelter is so needed," she said, trying a last argument. "It's worth the extra effort, the added work. Why don't you see that?"

"I won't argue the point, Ivy." Withdrawing his hands from his pockets, he stood straight, a stubborn set to his mouth.

"Never mind. I'm sorry I even suggested it."

"Let's talk about something else."

"As you pointed out a moment ago, I'm stretched pretty thin. I'm going to bed. I've got to be up early tomorrow."

"Tomorrow? Tomorrow is Sunday. You can sleep until midmorning and we can all go to the second service."

If that didn't sound as though he and Aunt Arletta had her tomorrow all planned out, she would run a ten-mile race.

"Well, you can do that if you want to." She folded her lips in an effort to keep a lid on her temper. "I have a breakfast meeting with the committee. I'll make the late service from there on my own, thank you."

Turning on her heel, she left him standing in the middle of the room without another word. She hated being out of sorts. Especially right before going to bed. She heartily wished Aunt Arletta had let her know that she'd invited Noah to sleep on their sofa. She could've...oh, at least mentally prepared herself.

Thirty minutes later, she lay wide-awake still wishing it. She punched her pillow for the third time in ten minutes. She felt decidedly put out with Noah, and the knowledge he lay sleeping just down the hall didn't help her peace of mind a bit. If he'd just gone home, she could put him out of her thoughts.

Why his refusal to help this organization nettled her so much, she couldn't understand, but it did. His attitude smacked of disapproval. How, when he exhibited such spiritual faith, could he not want to help these women in need?

Well, he had a right to choose what he did with his own time just as she did, and now that she'd begun with the project, she wanted to see it through. No skin off her nose if Noah wanted no part of it. It was his loss.

The next morning she rose early, slipping into the bathroom to shower and shampoo and out again in twenty minutes. She took her time styling her hair to fall loosely on her shoulders, then carefully applied her makeup.

Her clock radio showed almost seven. Gerry was picking her up at seven-thirty. She had time to glance at the morning paper. She liked keeping up with the retail ads; it was good business policy.

Beyond her door, she heard a soft, cheerful whistling of a contemporary Christian tune. Recalling the words of promise and assurance, it lifted her spirits. Or maybe it was the whistling. Her dad often whistled when he was in a happy mood. She heard the bathroom door close, and left her room.

The fragrance of coffee wafted through the hall

the minute she opened her door. Mmm...Aunt A was making the real stuff. Obviously, Noah was worth the time and bother of making a whole pot of regular coffee.

"Good morning, Ivy dear," Aunt Arletta greeted before opening the oven door. Her blue eyes sparkled with goodwill. Dressed in her purple sweat suit emblazoned with a rising sun printed in gold, she had argyle socks on her feet. Her hair corkscrewed around her cheeks with abandon.

"Morning, Aunt A." Ivy watched the pan of sweet rolls, topped with bits of real butter and cinnamon, go into the oven. Her mouth began to water. No bakery could touch Aunt Arletta's sweet rolls.

"Um, those are going to take a full thirty minutes, aren't they?"

"Just about."

"Then you have a few minutes to change, um..."

"Oh, Noah doesn't care how I look, Ivy. It's you who catches his eye. I'll change later."

Ivy sighed an "Okay" as she poured herself a mug of coffee and sat down at the kitchen table. It would be a race between Gerry's arrival and when the rolls would be done.

Noah emerged from the bathroom a few minutes later, smelling lightly of an outdoorsy aftershave. He wandered into the kitchen unhurriedly as though this were his usual morning routine.

Ivy peeked at him from around the cartoons she was reading. He wore a new sweater. Bright red over a solid dark shirt, it made his brown eyes look even deeper and somehow mysterious. How he could look so fresh after a short night on their sofa was a puzzle to her.

Spying her glance, he gave her a quick grin and a wink. Jerking her paper up, she ignored him.

"This is the day that the Lord has made," Aunt Arletta sang in her warbly soprano. "Let us rejoice and be glad in it..."

"It sure is. And it sure smells like heaven just made a deposit in your kitchen, Aunt Arletta. What have you got in the oven?"

"Oh, these are my breakfast sweet rolls," Aunt Arletta simpered. "Nothing that special, but I like to make them once in a while to keep my baking skills up to par."

Nothing special? Aunt Arletta had won three blue ribbons for her cinnamon rolls over the years from the state fair and other bake contests.

"Well, if you're looking for an appreciative customer for breakfast, I sure am glad you picked me." He snagged a chair from beneath the table with his foot and sat down. One long leg stretched all the way toward her, his black loafer nearly touching her high-heeled pump. "Find anyone you know in the funny papers Ivy?"

"Here, you can look for yourself." Ivy shoved the colored print his way and picked up another section.

She listened to him chuckle at one of the cartoon cats and turned the page. The oven dinged, Aunt Arletta grabbed oven mitts to remove the rolls, and the doorbell rang all at the same time.

"That'll be Gerry," she murmured. But she didn't think either of them cared; the two of them were intent on transferring the rolls to a platter, a good bit of teasing exchanged in the process.

"I'm glad you're on time," Ivy said, opening the

door. ''Please come in a minute. Aunt Arletta has a guest for breakfast, but I want you to meet her.''

''A breakfast guest?'' he said, a slow smile breaking across his face.

A sudden blush climbed Ivy's cheeks as she realized the connotation he'd put on her statement.

''Um, just that, Gerry. A guest who is, um, going to drive Aunt Arletta and her friend Shirley to church,'' she improvised. In truth, until she'd known Noah was to spend the night at their apartment, she'd assumed she'd drop Aunt Arletta and Shirley off at the church building before continuing to the meeting. She'd accepted Gerry's offer to pick her up as a way of introducing him to her aunt.

''They're ready,'' Noah said cheerfully, poking his head around the kitchen door. ''Hi, Gerry ol' buddy.''

Gerry's brows lowered. ''What are you doing here?'' His tone seemed to add a silent ''again.''

''I'm a guest,'' Noah answered brightly.

''He's the guest,'' Ivy muttered. ''But never mind, I want you to meet my aunt.''

Aunt Arletta came through from the kitchen. Her cheek smudged with icing and still pink from Noah's teasing, she looked a picture of a mischievous elf. Gerry's gaze went a little blank.

''Gerry, I'd like you to meet my aunt, Mrs. Arletta York.''

Gerry nodded. ''Nice to meet you, Mrs. York.''

''Oh, how do you do,'' Aunt Arletta said formally. ''Would you like a hot sweet roll and a cup of coffee?''

''Thank you, but I don't think we have time.''

''I'll just get my coat,'' Ivy said hastily. She grabbed her best blue wool coat from the hall closet.

''You don't know what you're missing,'' Noah said. ''I've already sampled one, and I can tell you, Aunt Arletta could compete with the White House bakers.''

Ivy turned around in time to catch Aunt Arletta's proud beam. ''Well, I have won a blue ribbon or two.''

''That's very nice, Mrs. York.'' Gerald remained unimpressed, but he didn't seem put off by Arletta's appearance, either. ''We should be on our way, Ivy, if you're ready?''

Ivy hid her relief. They were going to get out of the apartment before Aunt Arletta said anything outrageous.

She had been eager to introduce Gerry to her aunt. If he really wanted to see her more often, she thought it was best to have the introductions out of the way early. Her loyalty toward her aunt was solid.

''Are you going to make it to the eleven o'clock service, honey?'' her aunt asked as Ivy opened the door. ''It's one of the best of the year, in my opinion, where we thank God for the yearly harvest. I like to sit way up front so I can see all the little children bringing things to the Lord's table.''

''Well, yes...'' True, this was the Sunday before Thanksgiving, and she did want to give praise and thanks for her business increase.

''I hope next year at this time we can praise God for an increase in the family,'' Arletta continued. ''None of the Yorks are getting any younger, you know.''

Ivy felt the burn start at her neck and travel all the

way up to her hairline. She tried for a bright laugh, but accomplished only a feeble chuckle.

A funny, strangled sound came out of Noah before he muttered, "Right on, Aunt A." Ivy felt like strangling him for encouraging her aunt.

Glancing at Gerry, she gained no clue to his thoughts. She moved on quickly. "You don't expect the meeting to go beyond a couple of hours today, do you Gerry?"

"Probably not," he answered. "But I had thought..."

"Don't worry about Aunt A, Ivy," Noah pronounced. "I'll see she gets home. But we'll miss you at church."

They would, would they? Not likely. How could Noah assume she wanted to miss church entirely this morning? It was just as important to her to be in the worship service as it was to Aunt Arletta—she rarely missed a Sunday.

"Count on me, Aunt Arletta." She shot Noah a warning glance. "I'll meet you in our usual place."

"Down in the front, remember," Noah reminded.

In the parking lot, Gerry helped her into his expensive sedan and headed toward the Mission Hills district. "I'd hoped we might spend the entire day together, Ivy. Perhaps take in a gallery after the meeting broke up. Or there's a string quartet playing a matinee concert downtown we might attend. Then have dinner afterward."

"It all sounds lovely, Gerry." It did. She couldn't recall when she'd had a long lazy Sunday afternoon entirely free from some kind of task to be done. He described exactly the kind of day she used to dream of having with a perfect husband. When she'd had time to dream. It was tempting.

"I wish I could. But my days are so full that I have little time with my aunt, and Sundays..."

"It's all right, Ivy," he said after a long pause. "We'll try it again another time. Right now let's concentrate on our meeting at hand. Barbara told me after our last gathering that she liked your idea about holding an auction of celebrity clothing."

He slowed as he negotiated a traffic light, then turned to smile at her. "Let's kick that around with the others today. Meanwhile, if we're going to get the country club for a Valentine's Day Dance, we'll have to pull some strings, coming at it so late. They're booked up for most of next year already."

"Oh? Well, if they're already booked, we'll have to find another place."

"Not necessarily."

"What do you mean?"

"We'll talk to the management and see what can be done."

Ivy had never known anyone with that kind of influence. Could Gerry really get preferential treatment from the country club in the matter of a booking date?

Finally they reached the house where the meeting would be held. A circular drive led to a gracious entrance and a maid met them at the door.

The lovely house belonging to one of the committee members gave Ivy a feeling of total enjoyment. She cast an approving eye over the fashionable color scheme as they were led into a back breakfast room large enough to seat a dozen people. Toni Benton, the hostess, greeted her with warmth and Gerry looked pleased.

More than two hours later, she checked her watch. "I really hate to be the first to break away," she murmured apologetically. "But if we don't leave now, I'll be late for church."

Twenty minutes later, she thanked Gerry for the transportation, and slid out of his front seat. She'd invited him to join her, but he'd politely excused himself with an ambiguous "I'll call you next week. After the holiday."

She watched the car pull away, wondering if he really would. She'd been drawn into his world now, they'd be thrown together often over the next months with the work for Deborah's Dwelling and the decorating he'd commissioned. But did he really want to see her again? Personally? After this morning?

She turned to see Noah beckoning from the church foyer, holding the glass door open as she ran up the walk, his grin in place.

Ivy wanted to strangle him for sure.

Chapter Nine

The next morning, Ivy completed her arrangements with the Shears and Watson law office for their holiday display. Mr. Watson wanted the work done the weekend immediately after Thanksgiving.

Hanging up the phone, she stared at it a moment, tapping her fingers in annoyance. Noah and she shared the commitment, they had to share the work.

She was very put out with Noah, although she no longer wanted to strangle him after Gerry had called her Sunday evening just to wish her good-night. It gave her hope. But the fact remained, Noah seemed to show up altogether too often whenever Gerry made an appearance. It was off-putting. How long would any interested man like Gerry continue to ask for her company when he found another so often on the scene?

Sighing, she punched in Noah's number. Friday night or Saturday morning? Traditionally, it was the busiest weekend of the year. She really needed to be in the store both days, but she could leave Sherri in charge Friday evening.

"Friday night," she said into the phone right after she identified herself and her purpose.

"Sounds fine to me," Noah responded. "How long do you think it'll take?"

"Several hours. There's a lot to be done and since this is the first time to decorate these offices, I'm not sure what we may run into. But Mr. Watson approved my sketches and I've marked all the electrical outlets. If we can get Brad to come along, the work will flow faster."

"I'll call him. What time do you want us there?"

"Six. The office closes at five, but we want to give everyone enough time to clear out."

"Okay, I'll be there with the trees, roping and tools. Anything else?"

"Live poinsettias. A dozen. Traditional red."

Relieved to have that set up, she began to check her materials list one last time as she said goodbye.

"See you on Thursday," he said, jerking her to attention.

"Thursday?"

"Thanksgiving. Aunt Arletta invited me. I'm bringing a friend."

"Uh, that's...nice." She struggled to be gracious.

Only one friend? She shouldn't be surprised. In fact, their small apartment had held a dozen guests at Thanksgiving in years past. They overflowed the kitchen table to sit in the living room, and even on the floor. Somehow in Aunt Arletta's mind the holiday surpassed even Christmas for sharing a meal. "I'll see you then."

Barbara strolled into the shop on Tuesday. Hearing

Emily greet someone and realizing her clerk was already busy with another customer, Ivy stepped through into the store.

Ivy hadn't quite decided yet if Barbara really liked her store or merely wanted to gain her friendship to find out more of Noah's activities. Ever since that day Barbara had come upon Noah there, she seemed to think Ivy knew him much better than she did.

"Oh, hello, Barbara. What can I do for you today?"

"I had an hour to spare and I wanted to look at that angel sculpture you described a couple of weeks ago. You said it was unusual and I need a gift for a dear friend."

"Ah, of course." She turned and walked back toward the checkout counter. "Actually I have it here in the case behind the register. I wanted to protect it while placing it where customers were more likely to see it. It's so..."

Ivy handed the piece to Barbara and watched her face change subtly as she studied the sculpture.

"I see what you mean. It has an unusual quality. Ethereal," Barbara said with reverence. She touched the features with gentle fingers. "The artist is quite talented. Who is he, did you say?"

"I didn't. I don't actually know the artist. He's a friend of Noah's."

"Oh? I thought I knew all of Noah's friends," Barbara murmured, flipping her hair behind her shoulder. "At least I used to."

Then as if changing her thought abruptly, she reached for her wallet, saying briskly, "I'll definitely take this, it's wonderful. But would you find out who he is please? I'd like to see more of his work."

"Certainly. I meant to ask Noah more about him this morning, but his first name is Matt." At Barbara's curious glance, she hastily added, "Noah and I have a holiday decorating job to do this weekend and he mentioned Matt's name in passing."

Seeing that her information about time spent with Noah didn't seem to unduly ruffle Barbara, Ivy lifted her tone. "I'll ask Noah more about the artist on Thanksgiving."

"Oh?"

"Aunt Arletta asked Noah to share the day with us. My aunt loves having company and we always have a houseful of people on holidays. Especially on Thanksgiving..." At Barbara's rather blank stare, she added, "You'd have to meet my aunt to understand."

"Mmm...must be nice." Barbara chatted as she pulled a credit card from her wallet. "My parents have been gone about five years now. Killed in a plane crash in Europe. Never had aunts or uncles. Gerry's not into holidays much as family togetherness. He uses the time to make use of the resorts. In fact, he's out of town this week."

"I didn't realize he was gone," Ivy responded casually. "He didn't mention his plans to me. Won't he be back for Thanksgiving?"

"No. He's returning on Monday."

"I see. Well, what are you doing for the holiday?"

"Oh, I'm not really sure." Barbara was too elegant to give a shrug, but something in her voice gave Ivy the notion there had been a mental one. "I had thought to have dinner with a girlfriend, but she had a chance to, um, go elsewhere. I told her to take it.

Not every day comes along to meet a guy's family, is it?"

Barbara hid it well, but all at once Ivy thought she caught a little loneliness in the back of her gaze. Compassion for anyone alone on a holiday knocked at Ivy's heart. She'd been living too long with Aunt Arletta, she supposed, for her aunt's sensitive nature not to rub off, and Aunt A defiantly believed in the "Do unto others" and "Love your neighbor" directives.

"No, of course not," Ivy murmured slowly, thinking of the lonely day in store for her new friend. Barbara wasn't used to the modest kind of life-style Ivy lived, might not find their hospitality to her liking, but she took a deep breath and plunged ahead, just the same.

"Well, Barbara," she started cheerfully, "you must come to us for the day. You'll be very welcome. And Aunt Arletta cooks up a storm of a traditional meal."

Barbara gazed at her with a startled uncertainty.

"Ivy, you are a kind soul, but are you sure about that? I mean, shouldn't you check first with your Aunt about the seating arrangements or something?"

A chuckle bubbled up. If Gerry hadn't mentioned Aunt Arletta to Barbara, she had a new experience waiting for her.

"I'll tell her to set another place, but I don't need to check with Aunt A. She delights in the whole holiday thing. We'll eat in the middle of the day around one, and visit or take walks for the rest of the afternoon. But I warn you, it'll be very informal."

"In that case, I'd love to come."

The surprise was that Ivy was pleasantly surprised

at Barbara's ready acceptance. She wrote down the address, suggested a time, and rang up Barbara's purchase. This was bound to be a first for the young woman.

A first for Ivy, too. She wondered if Barbara really wanted to deepen their budding friendship or see more of Noah?

"Are we here?" Chad eagerly asked Noah from the back seat. The little guy seldom met new people and, this past year, he'd had little adventure or other type of break in a closely structured life. He knew far too much about a parent in pain and discomfort and adult concerns than most four-year-olds.

"Yep, we're here, tiger," Noah answered with a glance for Chad's dad, Matthew Moore. Matt's uneasy expression told him he'd better get this pair into the house before Matt had a chance to back out. Again. He'd done a lot of tall talking to get Matt to accept the invitation to Thanksgiving dinner from a stranger. "Now take it easy. Let's get your dad on his way, and then you can carry the flowerpot."

Noah climbed from behind the wheel of his friend Matt's van and hauled out the portable ramp from the back end. He'd constructed it last year to smooth Matt's path whenever he needed it. Matt, as insistently independent as always, opened his own door and swung his walker from the back seat beside Chad. Painfully slowly and with extreme care, Matt maneuvered himself out and firmly planted himself on the tarmac.

"Second building," Noah explained. They began the snail's pace toward their goal. "Chad, can you find number thirty-six?"

"Sure, Noah," the little boy chirped. "Number thirty-two, number thirty-four, number thirty-six."

Noah swung the four-by-six platform over the one step to the Yorks' door.

Chad knocked. Or rather pounded his small fist until the door swung open beneath the onslaught.

"Well, I guess you really want to come in," Ivy said, her smile bright and sunny when she spied the boy. Her quick glance took in him and Matt, too, and Noah felt his heart take a leap, something that happened regularly in Ivy's company. He only wished she'd offer him a little more than the same friendly encouragement she offered Matt and Chad. Or any romantic encouragement at all. She appeared far more romantically inclined toward Gerry, a matter that was beginning to get under his skin.

It wasn't mere masculine jealousy. At least, he didn't think so. He and Gerry had both been attracted to the same girl a few times in the past, egging each other on in their pursuit with friendly rivalry without it really mattering which of them the girl finally accepted. This time it was different. It wasn't that he and Gerry stood on opposite sides of a major life issue, either—one that had rent their friendship and given him many a night of deep thought. He just knew it wasn't the same.

Gerry wasn't the man for Ivy. He was. He'd known it since the night she'd fallen into his arms on the basketball court.

Ivy, however, wanted to keep him at arm's length. He had to figure out how to change that.

He was truly thankful that Aunt Arletta liked him. She was a peach. Arletta was a throwback to the kind of generous, warmhearted woman his grandmother would've understood and chosen for a friend. His mother would know what he meant. Arletta's eccentricity didn't bother him a whit. He enjoyed her antics and applauded her staunch loyalty. The woman could stand in the front battle lines in defense of any given issue concerning faith or family, and he gloried she was on his side.

He wished Ivy was.

Ivy, if she'd only relax a little, could find that same sort of balance in life her aunt owned. She took everything so seriously. She needed more fun in her life, more lighthearted exercise. She liked to pretend to be a hardheaded businesswoman, and although he thought her savvy enough to run a corporation or a whole string of stores, that outer shell covered a woman who was afraid to look too deeply at her inner softness. Or even show she had any. He'd asked Aunt Arletta why she was so guarded.

She'd been hurt enough to keep all her emotions locked away, Aunt A confided in him. It would take time and a mighty lot of patience for her to trust loving anyone again. Even the Lord waited for the day when she'd release it all and feel His joy again. That was the day for which Aunt Arletta prayed.

Noah's biggest prayer of late was that her affections would fall his way when that happened.

"Come in, please," Ivy invited with real warmth toward the guests he'd brought, thereby causing his own to blossom. By no expression or word did she show surprise at Matt's disability, and only delight at sight of the boy. Though he'd explained to Aunt Arletta about his friend Matt and his son Chad, he rather imagined Aunt A had failed to forward the information to Ivy. Perhaps she'd become immune to surprises from Aunt Arletta's direction.

Chad rushed through the door and thrust his pot of Christmas cactus into Ivy's hands. "This is...this is a cactus. It's for the ladies of the house. It really doesn't grow around here, Daddy says, but people like it anyway. I can read...."

Matt began his slow ascent over the threshold, his concentration bringing out sweat drops on his forehead. Noah remained patiently behind him until he was through the door.

Ivy didn't even blink at Chad's lightning change in directions. She did, however, back up to clear the entry for Matt.

"You can read? Already?" She smiled with a playful gleam in her eye. Chad had captured her heart in an instant, Noah suspected.

"You look awfully young to me to be reading," she added. "Don't you think so, Barbara?"

"Yes, he does," Barbara agreed.

Noah noticed Barbara Reeves for the first time, seated on a straight chair brought in from the kitchen. He wasn't above being caught by surprise himself, he thought, swiftly looking around the living room to see if Gerry was there as well. It would be like Aunt Arletta to invite him, since Ivy had been seeing a lot of him lately. But only Barbara, beautiful and sleekly dressed in blue wool slacks and silk blouse under an embroidered vest, occupied the room.

"Uh-huh. Daddy told me how," Chad told Ivy proudly. "Who's that singing?"

"That's my aunt," Ivy explained. "Would you like to meet her?"

Nodding, he then asked, "Why don't she come out here?"

"She will, eventually. But right now she's busy mashing potatoes, I think. And she has a rule. She doesn't come out until all her cooking is finished. I'm not even allowed in there unless I help set the table or something. I already did that, and I made a salad and green beans and sweet potato casserole, too."

"Oh," Chad said.

Matt stopped in the center of the room, his dark blue eyes sober as he glanced around him.

"Wow, it sure smell's like Thanksgiving," Noah said with a grin, hoping to ease his friend's feeling of awkwardness. "I hope there's pumpkin pie, too."

"You can take it to the bank," Ivy replied with a chuckle.

Noah swept both women with a glance. Ivy wore a forest-green sweater over matching slacks today, and over all that, an old-fashioned enveloping apron. She looked adorably domestic. "Ladies, this is Matthew Moore, the guy who's teaching me to carve. And my little buddy, Chad."

"You're Matt?" Ivy exclaimed.

"The artist..." Barbara murmured, her eyes wide.

"That's right," Noah said.

"It's awfully nice of you to invite us," Matt said, his anxiety showing. "Chad's been chattering like a chipmunk all week about coming."

"I want to see the lady who sings," Chad said, peeling out of a coat sleeve. Ivy reached for the coats and Noah handed his and Chad's to her.

Shirley bustled through the front door carrying a cardboard box fragrant with homemade dinner rolls.

"My oven isn't as even as your's, Ivy. I hope none of these rolls burned."

"I'm sure they'll be just fine, Shirley. Aunt A and I appreciate your lending us your oven." Ivy waved Shirley toward the kitchen, then called, "Aunt Arletta, Shirley has arrived."

"They smell wonderful," Barbara added and rose. She smiled tentatively. "Matthew, may I help you out of your coat?"

Noah took a step forward, knowing Matthew's usual grumpy response to too much coddling, but he got his second surprise in five minutes when Matt returned with a mere "Thank you" and allowed Barbara to shift his coat from first one arm and then another.

"Would you prefer a firm straight chair like this one or one of the lounge chairs?" Barbara asked as she handed Ivy the dark-blue wind jacket.

"I think the straight one, if you don't mind, thank you," Matt replied. "It's easier to get up again."

Barbara waited patiently while Matt seated himself. He took out his handkerchief and blotted his brow. Barbara hugged his coat to her chest and watched him with a fascination unlike her. Noah had never observed such intensity when he'd dated Barbara in casual fashion. Their relationship had been so pallid, after a few dates Noah thought it finally died simply of pure boredom between them.

"Here, let me take that," Ivy said, slipping Matt's jacket from Barbara's hands. Barbara scarcely noticed.

With six adults and one child squeezed around a kitchen table designed to hold only four people, Noah grinned as he frequently rubbed shoulders with

Ivy. He couldn't take a bite without feeling her presence at his side. When she rose to refill tea and water glasses, a whiff of the flowery cologne she wore drifted his way. When she passed Shirley's homemade pickles, the back of her hand brushed his. Her elbow accidentally poked his arm as she cut into a slice of turkey. He kept his own elbows tucked at his sides, giving him the humorous feeling of eating while bound by a straitjacket. What he really wanted to do was place his arm across the back of her chair, thereby giving them both more space—and bring on the possibility of more closeness.

Barbara, on his other side, gave most of her attention to Matt. Chad sat between Arletta and Shirley, basking in the spoiling he received.

"Aunt A and Shirley are having a great time with Chad," Ivy leaned a few inches his way to remark. He noted the exact curve of her mouth, a tiny bread crumb lingering on her bottom lip, and longed for the right to lean over and…

"Thanks for bringing him along," she continued as he jerked his gaze up to meet hers. "Aunt Arletta adores children. And holidays are just so boring without them."

"Chad is a charmer, sure enough." With resolution, he changed the direction of his thoughts. "He makes friends with most of the adults in his life."

"Well, I guess he can add a few more to his string." Ivy smiled and leaned even closer, lowering her voice. "I don't think Matt is doing too badly, either."

Noah glanced sideways to view only the back of Barbara's long blond hair. Beyond her, the lines around Matt's eyes were softer than Noah had seen them in the last year. Neither she nor Matt seemed aware of anyone else at the table.

He let a slow grin take over and turned it Ivy's way. "Never would've believed it, but there's no second-guessing the way the Lord will answer a prayer."

"How true, Noah dear. How true." Aunt Arletta, directly across from him, nodded in approval, though he thought she hadn't heard Ivy's remark. "Proverbs 16 verse 3 says, 'Commit to the Lord whatever you do, and your plans will succeed.'"

"What does that mean?" Chad asked. Arletta smiled and began explaining.

Noah shared his soft amusement with Ivy, watching hers in return.

"I don't believe I can face dessert after that lovely dinner," Barbara said later. Forks had slowly ceased to lift as conversation and good humor flowed.

"Me, either," Ivy agreed.

"We can save dessert until later," Aunt Arletta said. "Let's clear the table, Ivy."

"Uh-uh, Aunt Arletta," Noah spoke as he shoved back his chair. "You and Shirley have outdone the best cooks in the city today, and we all thank you. But Ivy and I are going to take care of the clearing away, right Ivy? And we're going to take a page from your book. We'll work better without anyone else crowding the kitchen."

"Oh." Ivy fluttered her lashes in momentary response, but recovered quickly. "Yes. Yes we are. Why don't you and Shirley go sit in the living room, Aunt A, and rest. Noah's right. We can whip through the cleanup in no time."

"If I sit down I'll fall asleep," Shirley murmured.

"Me, too. I know," Aunt Arletta said. "Chad, why don't you, Miss Shirley, and I go for a walk? There's a park a couple of blocks away with swings. You want to go?"

"Uh-huh. Can we go now?" Chad's glance toward his father held both eagerness and doubt. "Can I, Daddy?"

"Well, I—"

"We don't have to cross any major streets," Arletta said, reading Matt's hesitation. "And we won't let Chad get too rough-and-tumble on a full stomach."

"All right. Chad, make sure you wear your hood."

Barbara settled Matt in the living room once more while the two older women and Chad closed the door behind themselves.

Noah heard a television football game turned on; he paused, listening. In another moment the sound clicked off and he heard the soft murmur of voices. Ivy gave him a questioning gaze.

"What's wrong?"

"Nothing's wrong." He picked up a plate and began scraping. "I'm having a great time."

"Are you sure?" Ivy pulled out the dishwasher rack and loaded dishes as he handed them to her. "Does it bother you that Barbara seems interested in Matt?"

"Ivy, sometimes you have all the symptoms of becoming another Aunt A, do you know that?"

"Don't be silly. I—" She pursed her mouth, then broke out in a chuckle as she filled the sink with hot water and suds to wash the pots and pans by hand. "All right, I'm sorry I asked. I didn't realize I was prying."

"No, you wanted to know. It's okay. It's just that Matt has been through a bad time these past two years and I guess I'm thinking... I'm just surprised that Barbara has taken a shine to him. It's not her usual, uh, mode of operation. In fact, I was surprised to see her here today."

"Gerry is out of town. She was going to be alone today."

"Uh-huh! Just like Aunt Arletta."

"Huh!" She flicked water at him. "I don't think so."

He took the water full in the face and raised a threatening brow as he reached for a paper towel. "You want a water fight? Or a towel flicking contest?"

"Uh, no, I guess not." She gulped as he took a step toward her. Her eyes lit with laughter, and her mouth quivered with trying to smother it.

"I should warn you—" he moved closer "—I'm very good at water fights."

"I'm sure you are." She moved backward a step, her eyes widening when she came up against the refrigerator.

"I was a champion among my brothers," he murmured, placing his hands beside her head and leaning on his palms. He lowered his head slowly, letting his elbows bend, not touching her anywhere. Their noses were mere inches apart, their mouths only a bit more.

He waited a moment, giving her a chance to draw away if she wanted. But he hoped she wouldn't. He inched closer.

"I'll take a rain check," she managed to say just before his mouth met hers, softly yielding. It was the nicest kiss he'd ever had. The very nicest. He could only hope she felt the promise in his.

Chapter Ten

Ivy turned on her radio in hopes of hearing a few Christmas carols as she drove downtown. Decorative lights shimmered everywhere through the early misty night. She loved the few weeks during the holidays when buildings and houses joined the celebrations no matter what their faith. The lights dressed up the meanest of structures, made glowing wonders of the commonest lines. She recognized and loved the window candles which represented other faiths, too. Her heart expanded with a wonderful feeling of kindness and desire to give, to do something extra for everyone who crossed her path.

She turned toward the section of downtown that held the city hall. In this part of the city, few people still milled about. Most of them hurried to go home. Pulling into the alley behind the building where the law offices were located, she saw Noah and Brad waiting for her at the delivery entrance. Piled greenery peeked above the truck bed.

Ivy waved happily to see Brad, but smiled tentatively toward Noah. After that kiss on Thanksgiving day, she didn't want to be alone with Noah. She didn't trust his wayward, enticing smile. Or herself. Or the way he made her heart jump when she had no plans to fall in love with him. He simply didn't fit into her five-year plan. How could he fit into a lifetime?

Grabbing a cardboard box of materials and tools, she ran against the wind into the building, welcoming Brad's presence to keep the work session just that. She planned to activate all the professionalism she could muster to keep Noah at arm's length.

Mr. Watson, in late middle age with a receding hairline, let them into the tenth-floor reception room. Only a dim light from the front desk illuminated the area.

"Glad you folks are on time," Mr. Watson remarked. "I'm sorry I can't stay to see you through the evening, but I'm already running late. Foley, the building night man, is around if you need anything. Noah, if you could just see that everything is locked up after you leave, I'd be grateful."

"Sure thing, Mr. Watson," Noah answered. "Brad and I have to unload the trees and other supplies, so we'll ride down with you then come up the freight elevator." Turning, he flashed Ivy a quick smile, one filled with happy anticipation. "No need for you to come, Ivy. Brad and I can unload your stuff too."

"Thanks, Noah." She hesitated only a second before she tossed him her keys. Noah only wanted to be kind, she reminded herself. And helping her served both their interests. "I'll double-check the room layouts against my sketches."

Ivy straightened her blue sweatshirt and snapped on all the lights. She knew just where she wanted everything. The three stand-up carolers would go against the front-wall desk so they were the first display visitors saw when they came through the door. A bank of potted poinsettias went in front of them.

Brad and Noah arrived with a huge Douglas fir on a dolly. Ivy directed them to the conference room and showed them where it was to go. A few minutes later they came up with the green roping. An older man, dressed in a worker's uniform and whom she assumed to be Foley, followed with a stepladder.

The men made two more trips before they paused.

"That's everything out of your car, Ivy," Brad said, shedding his coat. "The boxes and these figures."

They all went to work. Noah and Brad headed back to the Douglas fir, Foley nodded after being thanked and muttered his way out. At seven-thirty, Foley returned, a pizza delivery man in tow.

"This fellah says somebody here ordered pizza?"

"It's all right, Foley. I ordered it," Noah said, coming forward. He paid the man along with a generous tip. He sniffed, his eyes closing in momentary pleasure. "I'm starved. How about you two?"

"As a matter of fact..." Ivy murmured, hoping he couldn't hear her tummy growl. It had been another one of those days when she hadn't had time to eat since a snatched roll for breakfast.

"Got things to do," Foley declined Noah's invitation to join them and ambled from sight.

Brad fetched colas from the vending machine in the employees' lunchroom and the three of them sat companionably on the floor opposite the Christmas tree with their backs to the wall and munched their way through supper. They said little. Ivy stared at the ten-foot tree. Only tiny blue lights had been strung yet. They twinkled through the branches like stars on a midnight sky.

"It's lovely the way it is," she said. "Something about the simplicity has a strength all its own."

"Yeah, it is," Noah agreed. He crossed his ankles and tipped his head to view the tree from different angles. "I don't like too much stuff on a tree. I prefer simple ones."

"A case of less is more?" Ivy asked, wondering if he applied his philosophy to everything in life. Was that why he was content to live in a trailer? Many people were happier in a self-contained unit than an apartment, she knew. She'd only known apartment living, but she wanted a house of her own one day. Did he never want anything more from his existence?

"Something like that," he answered, referring to her comment. "A few things enhance it. But you can't see the beauty of the tree when it's over-cluttered with decorations."

Brad got up to dump the pizza box and soiled paper towels into the trash, then disappeared down the hall.

She should return to work, too, Ivy thought. It was too easy to sit admiring the tree in cozy comfort with Noah.

He turned his gaze her way and continued his thought. "Like a garden. Overplanting or crowding not only chokes the life out of the flowers and bushes, but you can't really focus on the unique qualities of each species if all you see is a jumble."

"Yes, I see what you mean." She rose, heading back to her tasks at hand without telling him her plans for the tree. He'd see soon enough that their thoughts on design ran along the same lines. "If we keep up our pace we should be out of here by ten."

It was closer to midnight by the time they stood back to admire the finished work. Brad switched on the lights, and the metallic blue and silver bows, balls, and silver pine cones glowed with reflection, highlighting the natural tree. A nativity scene spread on velvet sat at its base along the curve.

"See what I mean?" Noah said in satisfaction. He hooked his thumbs in his back pockets. "The perfect balance. Perfect emphasis on why we celebrate Christmas."

"Wow! It's the best Christmas tree I've ever seen. Makes me feel...uh...like...uh, humble or something," Brad stammered through his reaction with embarrassment.

Ivy examined the colorful foot-high figures of Mary and Joseph and the cradle with Baby Jesus. The wise men and shepherds stood close by, reminding her of the wild hope and joy those long-ago men must have felt, and the staggering knowledge of God's love passed down through the centuries since then. A lump filled her throat. "Yes..."

Without intending it, she glanced Noah's way. His warm gaze gathered her in an invisible embrace, sweet and alluring and immediate, but most of all connected. A longing swept through her, something like the need of an hour before, but it wasn't a craving for food. It was a hunger from her heart. From her soul.

She turned away and began picking up her tools.

They admired the window swags with their matching designs as they retreated to the reception area. Satisfied with everything, Ivy pronounced the job done.

Reminding each other to drive safely home in the midnight hour, Ivy tried to ignore Noah's longing glance as they climbed into their separate vehicles.

"Gotta get Brad home," Noah reminded her.

"Mmm..." She switched on her motor. She refused to feel sorry for Noah's long drive home afterward. Inviting him to sleep on their couch mustn't become a habit. It bred too much familiarity, too much intimacy. Even though Aunt Arletta would do it. She'd take it in stride to wake in the morning to find Noah once again on her couch. She'd be proud Ivy had thought of how tired he must be and wanted to save him...give him...

"Um, Noah?"

In the act of rolling up his window, he paused. "Yeah?"

"Um, if you want to make use of our couch again, it would save you an hour's drive tonight."

A huge grin spread across his face. 'Thanks, Ivy. Think I will."

Now why had she gone and done that? Why couldn't she simply have let him go his own way? It was all too close for comfort.

Aunt Arletta would be happy. She'd assume Ivy had more romance than simple human compassion in mind.

Ivy groaned. She'd have to do a lot of tap-dancing in the morning. She couldn't allow either her aunt or Noah to believe that.

* * *

On Tuesday Sherri called in sick with a sinus infection.

"All right, take care of yourself, Sherri," Ivy said, already rubbing out Sherri's name on the day's schedule. "I'm sorry you feel so lousy. Let me know how you feel in a couple of days, please?"

Without her assistant, Ivy was confined to the store all day. It wasn't a problem, but she'd have to reshuffle the rest of her weekly schedule. She'd agreed to meet with the Deborah's Dwelling committee on Thursday morning. The store had to be covered.

Besides, Gerry had asked her to lunch after Thursday's meeting. She wanted to accept.

She called Tina. Her confidence in the nervous young woman hadn't improved, but she needed someone. She'd find someone else for Thursday.

But Tina mumbled out that she really didn't think she could work any extra hours. In fact, she had been thinking of quitting. She wouldn't be coming in at all.

"Are you sure?" Ivy asked, her heart sinking. "Can't you hold out until after Christmas?"

Tina insisted she was positive and asked for any remaining pay be mailed to her.

Ivy called Emily. At least Emily liked the work and showed an appreciation of the stock they carried.

"I'd like more hours, I really would," Emily responded. "But I haven't a baby-sitter."

Ivy thanked her and hung up. Perhaps Brad? The young man had never worked with customers, but he was personable and sharp. If she could team him with someone, if he had the free time, Ivy thought he might do very well. He wasn't home when she called, and she left word on his answering machine to call her.

A steady stream of customers filled the rest of her morning. Aunt Arletta called during a lull in the afternoon. Ivy bit her lip, tapped her pencil, then took a deep breath. She was desperate for help and explained her current need.

"Aunt Arletta, do you suppose you could handle a toddler for a few hours on Saturday morning?"

"I suppose so, Ivy. But I can help out at the store instead, if you'd like. Then Emily doesn't have to look for a sitter."

"That's a thought," Ivy responded, scrambling for a reason to refuse without hurting her aunt's feelings. "But, honestly, Aunt A, I think Emily needs the job. This way you'd be helping both of us."

"All right, if you think that's best." Yet Ivy could hear the disappointment in her aunt's voice.

"However..." Ivy slowly let her breath out.

"Yes?"

"I need someone here on Thursday morning for a couple of hours, as well. I think Brad might agree to come in." She prayed hard that it was true. "He can handle the register—" the modern register had been her aunt's horrified downfall "—if you can help with customers. How does that sound?"

"Thursday?" Aunt Arletta's smile came through the wire. "Certainly. You can count on me, Ivy dear."

"Yes, Aunt Arletta. I know I can." She only wished she could count on Aunt Arletta doing the reasonable thing in not insulting customers. Or messing with the accounts.

But when she returned early Thursday afternoon,

followed by a hopeful Gerry that she still planned to go to lunch with him, Ivy passed a young woman shoving her way through the front door with an angry mottled face. Her short coat opened on a red wool tunic that reached only to the top of long legs in black tights.

Ivy shot a gaze around the store. Aunt Arletta, wearing black athletic shoes under a felt Christmas skirt, was talking with an older, valued customer. Her first instinct was to rush over and disengage her aunt as she shoved a small wall plaque into the customer's hand. Brad stood nearby watching the departing young woman through the window, his face caught between amazement and amusement.

"What happened?" Ivy questioned Brad in a low tone, tipping her head toward the woman just disappearing from sight.

"Well..." Brad began, "Um, um, ah, your aunt..."

"What did Aunt Arletta do? Or say?"

"That girl bent over to look at those floor angels against the wall, and, um..."

"And?"

"Your aunt—she asked her if she forgot to put her skirt on this morning."

"Oh." Ivy felt her face flush and stole a look at Gerry. Aunt Arletta had her ideas about current fashions and wasn't afraid to voice them, either. As once before when he first met Aunt Arletta, his eyes looked a little glazed. Swallowing hard, she said, "Sorry, Gerry. I—I don't think I'll make lunch today."

"Yes. I see. Well, perhaps Sunday?"

"I'd love to. I'll call you, all right?"

"Do that, please. I need to talk with you Ivy. I'd like to speed up the work on Reeves House if you don't mind. And besides that, I'd just like to see you without a committee present."

"That's a lovely idea. All right, I'll clear my Sunday afternoon."

Ivy sent Brad to run Aunt Arletta home and rearranged the back display from her aunt's design. What would she do if Sherri couldn't come in tomorrow? Or if Emily didn't take to Aunt Arletta on Saturday morning?

It never dawned on her to question if Brad would be there on Saturday night to clean the floors. It was his usual night to do the thorough cleaning, and it took him several hours by the time he cleared and stacked things.

Then on Saturday night, she discovered her oversight. Her day had been long with steady shoppers. Sherri had come in, but left early. Ivy had manned the store on her own the last hour.

Outside the sky darkened even earlier than usual for the time of year, and quarter-size snowflakes began to drift down. It didn't seem to slow the steady flow of shoppers, though.

Toward six, Noah showed up. Customers kept her at the register for a time, but she realized he had begun to stack things out of his way in the back room. As soon as the customers left, she hurried there.

"What are you doing?"

"Taking Brad's place tonight."

"Why? Where's Brad?"

"He had something at school."

"He said nothing to me about it."

"Sorry, Ivy. I think he said something about Aunt Arletta giving him the okay. Anyway, she's the one who called me to help out."

Oh, fine. Now Aunt Arletta hired people and rearranged her work roster. "I'll have to speak to Brad about clearing things with me first from now on," she muttered.

"It's no sweat, Ivy." He gave her a what's-all-the-fuss glance. "I can handle cleaning a floor now and again."

"That's not the point, is it?" The front bell rang before she could make further comment, and she turned back into the showroom. She remained there until closing.

After she locked the front door and pulled the shade, she stood at the window a moment watching the snow come down. Steady heavy flakes. Already cars were slowing to allow for wet streets.

Only a few pedestrians hurried along, and one by one the other store lights flickered, either to a low night-light or out entirely.

Behind her, she heard Noah's steady progress. It was good of him to do the floors for her. He didn't have to step in for Brad; he could have let her struggle with either finding someone else to get them done or do them herself. She felt sorry now for acting so short-tempered.

The least she could do was buy him dinner.

Eating meals together had become a habit, she mused. But a habit she intended to put a stop to; it only encouraged him to think of themselves as a couple. She didn't want a repeat of that Thanksgiving kiss. She couldn't afford to let her emotions in for more of that kind of conflict. He was not Gerry.

But still, she could at least buy him dinner for doing her floors.

Chapter Eleven

"Thanks, Ivy, but I'll take a rain check," Noah said when she offered, catching her a bit off guard. She'd expected him to jump at the idea. "I've got to run out to check on Matt as soon as I finish here."

"What's wrong with Matt?"

"Don't know for sure. He's been in a blue funk lately. I'm hoping he's just in need of some company. Want to come with me?"

She considered the idea a moment. There was certainly enough to do if she wanted to stay another hour at the store, but it had been a long week and she was ready to close her doors.

"I think I will," she surprised herself into saying. "I owe him a check anyway. I don't have to wait until the close of the month to pay him, and with Christmas around the corner..."

"That would be nice of you, Ivy. Are you sure?"

"Yes, I'm sure." She stacked a set of children's Christmas-print bedsheets and pillowcases on a table. The wall behind displayed matching curtains. She'd been unsure about choosing the merchandise, but Emily had fallen in love with them and put a set on layaway for her little girl. Another set had sold this morning. "You must know that small vendors don't always have the backing to carry them through long periods. They need the quick cash flow.

"And I'd like to see the other angel faces he's carving," she continued, hoping her reasons didn't sound like mere excuses to spend more time in Noah's company. "I think we have a real market for them."

As she talked, Noah replaced the merchandise he'd moved, then rolling down his sleeves, he slowly came toward her, his eyes growing softer.

"Anyway," she murmured and gave the display a final pat. It seemed the obvious place to stop. She rested against the doorway to the back room, with her hands at her back. And completed her excuses—her reasons—for wanting to go along with Noah. "Aunt Arletta will probably be in the middle of her Saturday night TV shows with Shirley. I'll give her a quick call to let her know I'll be home later."

"All right. My car or yours?" he said with a mischievous grin. He placed his palm high against the door frame just above her head, his arm taking his weight. Just as he had on Thanksgiving. The light in his eyes gave her a buzz, and all at once the only thing she could think of was that kiss they'd shared. How sweet his lips felt on hers. How much she wanted to feel them...

How afterward she'd sworn never to let him kiss her again.

"Ah, mine. It's more comfortable than the truck."

A corner of his mouth indented.

Suddenly realizing how her comment sounded, she felt the flush heat her cheeks to her hairline. "I mean...um, I have to run by the bank and I don't think I can reach the automated teller..."

"Uh-huh, it's okay, Ivy. I remember your Saturday routine. All right. We'll use your car. But I'd like to pick up some ice cream on the way, okay?"

"Yeah, that'll work." But he made no move and he stood very close. His breath fanned her cheek.

"Perhaps I'll take little Chad something...." She made a rather scattered glancing survey around her store, trying to draw her thoughts together. Noah's close proximity unnerved her just a little too much. It simply wasn't fair to have this reaction when he was so...so unsuitable for her life plan. "I just don't have any toys, though. I know," she said, drawing a shaky breath as she pushed past him. "Bob, at the five-and-dime up the street, will still be just closing. If I hurry I can catch him and I can get something for Chad. Watch the store a minute, Noah."

She grabbed her coat, saying, "I'll just run up and see," over her shoulder as she almost leapt through the door. She scarcely noticed the thick wet flakes sticking to her hair and lashes or the slushing made by passing cars. She paid little heed to the slowing of traffic. The short block became even shorter as she ran it, her thoughts tumbling in a hard self-scold.

The time out of Noah's company was twenty minutes of putting all her barriers back into place. When had they crumbled, how could she have let them? Where was her self-control?

Her emotions were running riot! She felt sixteen again, with no defenses at all. She'd sworn never to let herself be vulnerable ever again. She couldn't afford to let her heart decide her fate.

Gerry. She had to concentrate on Gerald Reeves. She'd promised her Sunday afternoon to him, just the two of them. He was the man she wanted.

By the time she swung open the door at Wall's Intrigue, she was able to give Noah a benign, very bland smile. She held up a toy truck triumphantly. "I'll phone Aunt Arletta and finish closing up, then we'll be on our way," she promised.

"Good," he murmured with a beguiling grin. "I'll put away the mops and bucket."

She swallowed hard and shifted her gaze. Away from the soft, warm look in his.

The nightly bank drop took only a few minutes, but the grocery store detour took a bit more time than she'd anticipated. She waited in the car watching the snow come, hoping the streets remained clear until she was home for the night once more.

Noah came out with two bulging bags of groceries. Not only ice cream she thought, but made no comment. Following directions, she drove south to a small house in the old Waldo district.

"Just me," Noah spoke as they stomped the snow from their feet and stepped across the threshold. Matt moved back to let them in, surprise and doubt flickering in his eyes at seeing her.

"Noah!" Chad squealed with delight and wrapped himself around Noah's legs.

She hadn't thought about warning Matt of her coming with Noah. She bit at her lip, afraid she had embarrassed him.

"Hiya, tiger! Have you been a good boy today?" Noah swooped the boy up in his free arm to stroll out of sight around a wall that apparently separated the kitchen from the front of the house.

"I brought you some ice cream if you ate all your supper," she heard him tell the boy. She stayed where she was while the bag of groceries she held grew heavy, hoping Matt would say something more than just hello.

"Uh-huh, I did," Chad answered. "Ask Daddy. He didn't, though."

"We'll have to do something about that, won't we?"

"Matt, I hope you don't mind my coming along with Noah," she said low, so as not to upset Chad. "I should've called."

"It's all right, Ivy. Noah did call. He just didn't say he was bringing company."

"Well, he was cleaning my floors, you see, and I— Well, I thought," she stammered while she withdrew his check from her shoulder bag, "you might like your check before the end of the month."

"That's wonderful, Ivy." His face instantly lit up. "Yes, I can use it. We won't have to line up the candles after all," he joked as he sat down heavily in a worn armchair.

But Ivy had the suspicion the joke wasn't too far off the mark. The groceries in her arms didn't feel quite so heavy anymore.

He took in the amount of the check, his eyes growing wide as he stared at her. "Is this right, Ivy? Those little stables can't have been worth all this."

"Not the stables, Matt. In fact, I haven't totaled those yet. Sorry. No, this is from your angel head."

"Really? Someone liked it this much?"

Noah came back through and took the groceries

from her. "Yeah, Matt. I told you she liked it. Sold it real fast, didn't you, Ivy?"

"That's right. And Matt, if you have any more, I'd like to see them."

"I do, Ivy, but that was my best. I hoped...but I never thought it would... Are you sure?"

"Why, yes, why wouldn't I be? I'm a businesswoman, Matt. I made my percentage on that piece."

"You did? Oh, of course you did, how stupid of me." He brushed a hand across his eyes. "I just can't imagine someone paying that amount of money for something that comes so easily to me. Here, let me show you my other work and—" He struggled to rise so suddenly he almost tipped himself over. Then he paused, as if struck by a wayward thought. "You are telling me the truth, aren't you? It's not some form of pity?"

Ivy flashed a glance toward Noah. He made a helpless gesture as though to say he'd been through this argument before.

"Matt, I just pointed out to you that I'm a businesswoman. I can't afford to indulge in pity. It does no one any good." She didn't enlighten him that, to her mind, useful action was the form of help she'd learned at her dad's knee and her aunt's. "No, that piece is simply stunning. If you haven't recognized your talent yet, let me assure you that it's real."

Matt nodded, grinned ruefully, then beckoned her toward a side door. It led into the garage, fitted into a workshop. It took only a glance for Ivy to know he spent many hours here. He showed her more of his work.

"This was my first one."

"Mmm... Where have you studied, Matt?"

Bitterness and a sense of self-mockery threaded his low laughter. "I didn't study at all except through books I found in the public libraries. Never had time, never had any patience for it. If you don't think this one is good enough—"

"No, Matt, that's not it!" Ivy glanced hopefully at the half-opened door. Where was Noah? "This angel has a quality all its own. I know someone who may want it."

"You think someone would buy that one?"

"Yes, I think so. Are there others?"

"I have a couple of playful cherubs. I used Chad as my model."

Noah joined them. "How's the work coming, Matt?"

"Better. Ivy thinks she can sell more of it."

"Yes, and I also think I may have sold your first one too cheaply." She started to tell him who had bought the piece, but felt a tug of doubt. If he didn't ask, she thought it better for his pride not to say. "Matt, I'd like to be your designated dealer, but I have to be honest with you. I think your talent deserves a wider showing than what I can give it."

"I'll leave it to you, Ivy, I don't want to meet anyone else. Can't Noah and you take care of all that between you?"

Ivy glanced at Noah. He gave her a slight nod. "Yes, I suppose we can, but—"

"That's the way I want it," he insisted before she could put forth an argument.

They talked a bit more and by the time Noah suggested they leave Ivy noticed a real change in Matt's spirits. Bundled up against the bad weather they called goodbyes to the plaintive Chad who, after begging Noah to stay just a little longer to play trucks with him, now stood forlornly in the doorway clutching the toy she'd given him. Noah promised to return in a day or two.

The snowfall had thickened, covering her car rapidly. Ivy searched for her scraper and a long-handled brush, then finding an old pair of snowboots she kept in her trunk, pulled them on. She started the motor and wipers at the same time.

Glancing back once more at the house, she saw Chad's face pressed to the old-fashioned picture window. It gave her heart a twist to see such loneliness.

There was an odd set to Noah's mouth. Then she knew; he, too, hated leaving the little boy in such a state.

Ivy kept her gaze glued to the narrowing strip of pavement. The streets had grown much slicker during the hour or so they'd visited with Matt and Chad. The car handled more gingerly.

"I'm not at liberty to discuss Matt's problems with you, Ivy," Noah said when she asked why Matt felt so strongly about not meeting people. "He wants to keep his life private."

He yanked a tissue from the box she kept on the floor and wiped the melting snow from his face. "I took a chance on upsetting him by bringing you along tonight. Luckily, he seemed okay with it. Especially since you like his work so much."

"Like it? I love it. I just wish I had more contacts for him. But he obviously needs more help than he's getting and I don't understand..." She covered another block slowly.

Noah remained unusually quiet. She thought about

the situation she'd just witnessed. "You weren't just doing a grocery run as a favor, were you, Noah?"

He didn't answer.

"Admit it," she said as she turned onto another side street. "Those groceries were necessary."

"Watch the road, Ivy. That car up ahead has stalled on that hill."

They slowed to a crawl. Then stopped. The compact vehicle ahead of them came sliding down the hill backward, barely missing a parked car. It slithered to a halt only yards away. Another sat almost crosswise halfway up, its wheels grinding.

That hill was the shortest route to her store where Noah's truck was parked. Of course, she could turn and take a long circular way there, but the wiper blades worked more slowly against the heavy dense snow with each passing moment. It was coming down harder than ever, and they were much closer to her apartment than the store. Doing the sensible thing, like taking Noah home to sleep on her couch once again shouldn't bother her all that much, surely. It now seemed a habit, and what was it they said about familiarity? She only hoped it to be true. A little contempt for him might just be what she needed to cool the growing flutters he gave her. Besides, Aunt Arletta was always delighted to see him.

"Um, Noah..."

"Just a minute, Ivy. I think this car ahead needs help."

Noah shoved his way out of her car and strode through the ankle-deep white stuff. After talking to the driver a moment, he directed Ivy to back up, and then the other driver. Halfway up the block, the third car still spun its wheels. A truck arrived from the cross street, slowed and stopped. Noah and the truck driver conferred, then on foot, they both approached the farthest car.

Ivy watched while her car idled. She debated whether to turn off her motor and wait or…keep it running and wait. Or get out and try to help?

Backing her car to park against a curb, she shut off her motor and pushed open her door.

Noah and the truck driver took on dim shapes as they put their shoulders to the rear of the car and pushed. It took several tries for the car to get going again. She hauled in a sigh of relief and kept her gaze riveted on the two as they walked and slid their way back down the street, heading for the car in front of her. Their voices came to her in muffled tones.

Noah was a Good Samaritan. It came as no surprise for her to think of him in that way. Lord knew, she'd had enough examples. But the lessons hit home as never before.

Gerry was charitable too, but he went through channels and procedure. He had enough time and energy left over for a decent life.

She no longer needed the old saying about what familiarity bred. Her head was very much in control.

Chapter Twelve

"Here, let me drive," Noah commanded when he returned to the car after watching the last vehicle make the hill. The truck driver waved and went on his way.

"What makes you think you can do any better than I can?" Ivy snapped. She leaned back against the driver's door.

"I've driven some mountain roads during bad weather. Lived through a couple of Chicago winters." He lifted her away from the side of her car with ease. "You're a bit of a timid rabbit behind the wheel, Ivy. Now get in. I'm driving."

Timid! She? How dare he! She was a cautious driver.

"I don't think so," she began, grabbing his arm.

Noah chuckled and tightened his hold, bringing her up against him. Snow dropped from his cap to plop onto her nose. Without intending to, she giggled. In the scant streetlight, his dark eyes took on a teasing glow.

A flickering flash reflected in her window, alerting her to another car behind them. A police car crept up beside them.

"Everything all right here?" came a deep masculine voice. The face staring at them was craggy and solid, but not particularly old. He looked them over carefully but didn't get out of his car.

"Oh, um...yes, everything's fine, officer," Ivy answered.

"That's good," he replied in a tone that retained a slight suspicion. "But I think you should find another place to park. Better yet, take your, uh, discussion inside, why don't you? This hill becomes dangerous during bad weather."

This policeman thought they were that kind of parked? But that was ludicrous, Ivy fumed. She was a grown woman, not a teenager. And she had never "parked" in her life, even with Eric, even while a kid.

Taking a quick glance into Noah's face, she saw his mouth indent as though working hard to keep his laughter in control. It sparked something deep in her middle, a sense of silliness, of innocent but ridiculous fun. A sound erupted from her throat, somewhere between a snort and a chuckle. Caught between embarrassment and her own laughter, she had to swallow hard. Thank goodness, it was too dark for anyone to see her face properly.

"We're not waiting out the storm, officer," Noah answered in a breezy way, slipping his arm loosely across her shoulders. "We simply stopped to help another motorist up that hill. We're on our way home."

"Good 'nuff." The officer pursed his mouth. "Be careful, now."

"Right," Noah said. Without waiting for Ivy to respond, he slid into the driver's seat. Ivy glared at him. How dare he take advantage of the situation to win his argument? It didn't help matters when he ignored her by turning on the motor. It sat humming while the police car backed up to give them room, then waited.

Ivy bit her lip, but decided their argument could wait until they got home. She really had no choice without making a scene. Besides, she was getting cold.

Marching around the front of the vehicle, she climbed into the passenger side and slammed the door. She stared straight ahead. She'd just let Noah feel her irritation. See if he could tease her into humor again, she silently challenged. She'd find some way sometime, to let him know she was an independent woman who could take very good care of herself, thank you very much.

Noah put the car in gear and pulled into the middle of the street. Behind them, the policeman signaled them to stop again. What now? Noah braked gently.

The officer exited his car, flashlight in hand, and came forward.

"Ma'am, may I see some identification, please?"

"Why, certainly." Ivy dug into her purse to find her driver's licence.

"And you, sir."

"Sure thing, officer. Did we commit a violation?"

"Don't think so, sir. Just want to check something." He accepted Ivy's licence, glanced at her picture and then back at her. "Okay, Miss York. Wanted to make sure it was you."

"What do you mean?" Ivy questioned.

The officer didn't answer immediately, but made a quick glancing survey of the car's interior, then took the card Noah handed over. He studied it with care. "Is everything all right with you?"

"Yes, certainly," Noah answered in his velvety way. "What's the problem, officer?"

The officer checked the picture against what he saw in Noah's face, then handed them both back.

"Sorry. Your aunt called the station, gave us your plate number, and—"

"Oh no! She didn't!"

"Yes, ma'am, she did. You should stay in better contact with her Miss York, if she's the sort to fret. Our lines are busy enough without flaky...well, you know."

"Sorry, sir. I'll speak to my aunt about it."

"We're on our way home now," Noah assured. "We've only been delayed by the snow."

"All right. Take it easy, though. Don't want to have to answer another dozen calls."

A dozen? Surely he exaggerated. But Ivy couldn't be sure.

Her irritation with Noah evaporated as they crawled their way home. They saw a dozen cars abandoned on road shoulders, crazily parked on a grass verge, or even half blocking a street. Noah drove with careful but steady aggression, his hands firm on the wheel.

He didn't even ask; he took the quickest way to her apartment.

"Oh, my dears!" Aunt Arletta greeted them

dressed in her red robe, her soft face a pale blur. "Oh, mercy, I am glad to see you. The Lord be praised! When I talked to the police sergeant—"

"Aunt Arletta," Ivy said, stamping the snow from her feet. "You didn't have to do that!" She felt caught uncomfortably between wanting to scold her aunt for bothering the police and her own embarrassment. Instead of expressing any of those emotions, she took the older woman into a warm hug. "I told you I was delayed."

"But I was that worried for you in this snow." Aunt Arletta closed the door behind them. "Now mind you, the two of you stand right there on that rug to shed your coats and boots."

Like children, Ivy and Noah did as they were told, shaking out of their outer things while caked snow began to melt around their feet. Aunt Arletta fetched a couple of towels as she continued.

"Even the weatherman didn't expect this much snowfall and when I talked to the police the second time, they said it was bad all over and to be patient. But I didn't hear from you after you left the store and—"

"She was with me, Aunt A," Noah interjected, as he fluffed the towel against his hair, leaving it in dark spiky strands.

"Yes, but you know, anything could've happened. The TV said there were lots of accidents, and they're telling people to stay home unless it's an emergency." Aunt Arletta's hand flew to her cheek. "Oh, dear. You don't suppose they'll cancel church tomorrow?"

"It will take more than a big snowfall to close our church doors, Aunt Arletta." Ivy thought it wiser to ignore how many accidents there had been, and how many stalled vehicles. "How many times did you call the police, anyway?"

"Oh—" her aunt waved a hand in the air "—only, um, you know..."

Ivy sighed. "The local police from our neighborhood station knows Aunt Arletta by name and sight," she told Noah. "I'm only surprised the officer who stopped us didn't recognize us on first sight."

Noah chuckled. "They get lots of calls from nervous people, Ivy. They can handle Aunt A."

"I'm sure they do, but we're likely to get a citation for disturbing the police. Last year we had a rash of juvenile robberies in the neighborhood and she called three or four times a week for a month with her thoughts on the mystery. They, ah, didn't appreciate her, um, 'clues' or help in the matter."

"Then they've merely underestimated her astute observations," Noah defended with a grin.

Ivy shot him a don't-encourage-her stare. He merely chuckled. That was all she needed to add more clutter to her life, Ivy silently fussed—a man who became bossy in the trenches, demanding to take the driver's seat, and thought her aunt cute while Ivy had to deal with all the fallout of her aunt's actions.

Aunt Arletta preened under Noah's praise. "I don't know, Ivy. I think some of my thoughts on that string of robberies were quite valid. And they did appreciate my best brownies. Enough to invite me back for open house last summer."

"Well, I've put off getting a mobile phone because the store isn't that far from home," Ivy muttered with a sigh, deciding it was time to ditch her objections. ''And usually I have easy access to one. But now I think I should get one.''

''That's a good idea, Ivy,'' Aunt Arletta said, her white hair bobbing with a nod. ''Then I could find you no matter where you are.''

Ivy sighed again. She suddenly felt too tired to think about it.

''Well, I must call the police back and tell them you're home safe and sound and all. Noah, you're not going back out in this tonight, I should hope.''

''Nope, no way. I left my truck at the store.''

''Aunt Arletta, I don't think the police need another call just to tell them I'm safe. Besides, the officer who found us knows.''

''Oh, but I couldn't let them continue to worry, dear. I'll just keep it short.''

Ivy turned away and closed her eyes tightly for a moment. Then glancing at Noah, she decided to face the practical needs. ''I'm starved and I'm sure you are, too. But you're on your own to find your blankets and sheets. You know where they're kept.''

Aunt Arletta had just hung up the phone when it rang. Leaving it for Ivy to answer, she bustled into the kitchen. ''I'll find you two something to eat, Ivy, you don't have to bother. Noah, you just sit down and rest. I'll bring out your sheets and blankets.''

Now that made her feel a bit less than gracious, Ivy fumed as she grabbed the phone. Aunt Arletta loved spoiling Noah, but she didn't want him to grow all that used to it. He was taking too much for granted already.

''Hello.''

''Ivy?'' Gerry's low tone held a note of anxiety.

"I was becoming concerned for you. I couldn't reach you at the store and your aunt said you were past due home. This weather is quite treacherous."

"Oh, dear. I forgot to tell you Gerald Reeves called," her aunt yelled above the rattling of pans from the kitchen. "Twice."

Noah's eyebrows shot up. Ivy turned her back on him.

"I'm sorry, Gerry. I just came in. Will this weather make tomorrow impossible?"

"So did Kelly!" her aunt hollered. "Once."

"No, not at all," Gerry said smoothly in her ear. "I have a four-wheel drive for weather like this."

"She wants you to call her about the young adults' Christmas progressive dinner," Aunt Arletta called the final message from the kitchen.

"You do?" she answered Gerry. Noah had picked up a magazine and seemed to be absorbed in it. "Oh, have you been out helping the hospitals and emergency people? They usually put in a call for anyone who has heavy vehicles to help out."

"Uh, no, it, uh, hasn't been necessary. I just wanted to check on our time for tomorrow. But I'll have to cut our evening short. I have to fly to Switzerland on Monday morning."

"Oh?" Determined to hide her disappointment, she kept her voice light. "Will you be gone long?"

"About ten days, as it has worked out. Business, of course, but mixed with a few days of pleasure. As long as I'm there, I may as well stay through Christmas."

"Christmas in Switzerland? It sounds lovely." Mountains and old world charm. What an exciting place to spend Christmas. A part of her was instantly envious and a part of her felt disappointed that she wouldn't see Gerry over the holiday. And she remembered how lonely Barbara had been Thanksgiving without her only living family member. Where would she spend Christmas? Ivy couldn't imagine Christmas without Aunt Arletta.

"I wanted to ask you, Ivy, if you'd take over as chairperson of the Deborah's Dwelling committee while I'm gone."

Surprised at the request, all thoughts of a Switzerland Christmas flew out of her head. She let her gaze wander to Noah. He wasn't really reading that magazine, she noted.

"I'm flattered you think I can, Gerry. But what about Barbara?"

"Oh, I don't think Barbara is quite up to it. She'd only make a botch of things and she's no good with figures. I know I can trust you. You have such great organization skills, and you can always delegate."

"Well, surely most of the business to be done can wait until you return? It is your baby, after all. I'm still a newcomer to this."

Noah's fingers flipped a page. It rattled in the quiet room.

"But why should it wait, dear Ivy, with you there in charge to see that events move along? I know you can handle this, Ivy. Then when I get back we can enjoy the smoother ride."

"Well, I suppose I can." Surely she could manage to check on the progress of the committee members by phone, which was really all the time she had to give it just now. People were going to be busy with the holidays, anyway. Not much would be accomplished until after the festivities were over. "When do you return?"

"Not sure, exactly," Gerry replied. "Had to leave that open. But I'll keep in touch."

He didn't elaborate any further and quickly ended his call.

"Gerald, huh?" Noah asked casually.

"Yes." She removed her earrings and laid them on top of the bookcase which held the phone.

"You seeing him tomorrow?"

"Mmm-hmm."

"Seeing quite a bit of him, are you?"

"I'm involved in committee work with him. I told you about it, remember? He's asked me to take over for him while he's out of town."

Obviously, Gerry was one man who didn't see her as helpless.

Noah tossed the magazine aside. "You're not going with him, then?"

"No. Where did you get the idea I was?"

"Oh, I thought he might ask you, that's all. Never mind. What's so special about this shelter, anyway?"

Now why would Noah conclude that Gerry would ask her to fly to Switzerland with him? Did he know something she didn't?

"Older women, women who haven't any other avenues of help. Why don't you hop on board, Noah?" she asked, although he'd said no before. "We could use your help, especially after the ball really gets rolling."

"I don't think so, Ivy." He stood, and headed toward the kitchen. "As I've told you, I haven't any time for tea parties and society dances."

Ivy let a half-irritated sound escape her. It seemed

to her that Noah had turned his back on this project just because it was the pet charity of the Reeves family. And she didn't know the reason.

"You don't have to go all humble on me, Noah. It isn't just social affairs, you know. It's a lot of hard work."

"It's early in the game, yet," he said, implying a wait-and-see attitude. "You have no idea if it will bear fruit."

"Yes, it's in its early stages yet while we're still raising funds, and it takes time to do all that, but Gerry has been talking with some of the corporate people for sponsorship."

"I bet he has," he replied over his shoulder.

"What does that mean?"

"Nothing." He turned on his heel, staring at her a moment with his thumbs hooked in his back pockets. "Go on."

"Well, the search committee is looking for a suitable house that can be properly licenced and fitted out which requires working with real estate people, and then there's the hammering out of how the actual running of the place will follow."

"Uh-huh." He tipped his head at her, his eyes half closed. "Who's doing all this work? Who's making policy?"

"Gerry and Barbara have been doing most of that."

"Mmm..."

"Why do you say 'mmm' in that tone of voice?"

Aunt Arletta brought in a tray of sandwiches and soup, asking God to bless it as she walked. "Sit down, Noah, and relax. I won't bother you, children.

I'm going to listen to the news just a little while longer. In my own room. With the door closed.''

Well, if that wasn't subtle, Ivy fumed. Her aunt had never been so accommodating before when she brought dates home. In fact, she'd made herself a real nuisance at times.

''What tone of voice?'' Noah eased himself back down on the sofa and patted the empty space beside him.

''Disapproval,'' Ivy responded, ignoring his invitation to sit beside him. She took the armchair facing, and reached for a sandwich. After a moment, she asked, ''Why don't you like Gerry and Barbara?''

''I haven't said I dislike Gerry and Barbara, have I?''

''You might as well have. You and Gerry bristle like a couple of squirrels competing over the same chestnut tree every time you're in a room together, and you hardly said a word to Barbara while she was here on Thanksgiving.''

''Oh, I called you a timid rabbit, so now I'm a squirrel?'' He laughed.

''If it fits.''

''And I wasn't rude to Barbara on Thanksgiving.''

''Well,'' she conceded as she tucked her feet up under her ''not exactly. But you didn't bother to talk to her very much, either.''

''I don't think she missed Chad's and my scintillating conversation,'' he said with a grin, referring to the fact he'd paid more attention to the child. ''I thought Matt took most of her focus.''

''That's true, but you're sidetracking the issue.'' She snuggled deeper into her chair. ''What do you have against the Reeveses?''

"Look, Ivy," he responded with a frown. He no longer seemed amused as he leaned back and brushed his damp knees. "I've known Gerry and Barbara since—"

He stopped and looked away, then began again.

"Our parents knew each other a long time ago before the Reeveses' parents died. Gerry and I, um, crossed paths in college and sometimes ran in the same circles. That's all. It's just that we haven't anything in common anymore. Barbara..."

"You and Barbara were an item once, weren't you?"

"We hung out together."

"Did you quarrel?"

"I don't want to get into this, Ivy."

That was fair enough. She didn't like talking about her failed relationships, either. Whatever he and Barbara had once meant to each other no longer mattered. It was their business.

She was interested in Gerry, anyway.

Of course she was.

Gerry was the kind of man she wanted. Noah... Well, Noah was a kind man. A good man. A good friend, even, she had to admit. But—Noah was still a gardener.

"But you still refuse to get involved in forming Deborah's Dwelling"

"Leave it alone, Ivy. I'm not going to discuss this any more."

"All right." She swung her stockinged feet to the floor and rose. "That's fine with me. I'm going in to listen to the news with Aunt Arletta."

Chapter Thirteen

Noah woke slowly to soft kitchen sounds from inside the apartment. He rolled over. Diffused light told him dawn had arrived. He blinked rapidly, trying to bring himself more fully awake.

His wallet, change and comb lay scattered over the lamp table. His keys and a couple of folded notes decorated the carpet.

He listened to the sounds in the kitchen, hoping it was Ivy. He liked seeing her in the morning still sleepy-eyed, with mussed hair, her face free of makeup.

He wanted to tell Ivy that, but somehow the right time had never occurred. And now he had an unsettled notion he'd lost ground with her last night during their quarrel.

His shoulders bunched with tension. She liked Gerry altogether too much for comfort.

He let his breath stream out, long and slow. He couldn't blame a woman for liking Gerry; he liked Gerry himself. Yet their differences had led to a rift in their friendship and he didn't want to get into that with anyone except the Lord.

Patience, that's what he needed now. His feelings for Ivy made him just about crazy. He longed to tell her how much he cared but the time was just not right. She was the first woman who had ever made him feel that way. It puzzled him at first. Until he realized she was the woman whom he'd prayed for God to bring into his life. Now he prayed for Ivy to reach the same recognition he had.

Soon, please, Lord. Please clear up Ivy's doubts about me and any misdirection toward Gerry soon.

He rose with the fragrance of coffee, and wrapped himself in the terry robe Aunt Arletta had loaned him. Peeking around the kitchen door, he spied the older woman. "Good morning, Aunt A. The scrapers are out early."

"Thank goodness they are, but it's not all that early," she replied. "It only appears so because it's still snowing."

He gazed from the kitchen window. It didn't appear they had a sky this morning, only a gray ceiling.

"The early service has been canceled for today," Aunt Arletta continued, "but when I called the church secretary, she said they would hold the eleven o'clock worship as usual. And the TV weatherman said it should stop by midmorning. Surely the roads will be cleared enough by then, don't you suppose?"

"Oh, the road crews have been out all night," he replied. "I'm sure we can get there."

"Actually, the later service is just fine by me. I wanted to hear William preach this morning anyway." Aunt A spoke of their senior pastor, whom she never addressed with his formal title of Dr. Parker. "I'm in the mood to hear a rousing good sermon of how the world's need for a savior two thousand years ago is the same today. He usually gives us that kind of perspective sometime in December."

"In that case, I'll go out and start clearing the car of snow as soon as I have coffee."

"Oh, Ivy's already doing that."

"She is? I didn't hear her leave."

"About fifteen minutes ago."

"So I guess I'd better get along." He rushed into the bathroom to dress, and was out the door in five minutes. Everything in sight held nearly a foot of wet snow. The air had a sharp edge to it; temperatures were dropping, Noah guessed, which would make for icy conditions later.

He slogged his way to the parking lot, spotting Ivy's car just where he'd parked it. But he couldn't see Ivy. Then suddenly, clumped snow showers burst this way and that from behind the vehicle and he guessed her to be hidden from view.

Bending, he gathered a palm full of snow and formed it into a snowball. A perfect sphere, he hefted it a moment wondering how mad she'd be if he lobbed it. She wasn't often in a playful mood.

It was too much temptation. Knowing the snow cushioned the sound of his approach, he rounded the car and let it fly. She stood just as it reached her, landing against her shoulder and the side of her bare neck. Instantly startled, she spun around and stared at him.

"Oh, you—you—" The old-fashioned iris-blue stocking cap she wore sharpened the blue in her wide eyes, while her hair curled around its edges, framing her face.

Her small chin worked in agitation. She wiped the icy wet from her neck while she made a quick assessment, her eyes narrowed.

Then lightning quick, she used her long-handled brush as a scoop to fling snow at him from the top of her car. He watched it land at his feet, far short of its intended goal.

She also watched it fall apart without hitting its mark.

Her gaze lingered at his feet for a second before a disgusted expression flashed across her face. Noah couldn't help himself. He laughed. Out loud. Loudly, in fact.

"So that's it, huh?" Outraged, Ivy reached for more snow, but this time she molded it into a proper missile. "You think you can stand there without repercussions after you made a sneak attack?"

She launched the snowball and grabbed for more snow.

Laughing harder, he backed off, an arm raised to protect his face. She reminded him of a life-size jack-in-the-box as she bent and rose in rapid succession, snow forming a ball between her palms each time. The missiles kept coming.

"Now, now, 'Love thy neighbor,'" he quoted through his chuckles, refraining from any return fire. Her snowballs weren't solid enough to hurt a fly sitting still. His, he knew from past experience, could be packed so firmly they were deadly.

"Uh-huh. And whatever happened to 'Do unto others'? What's the matter, Noah? You can't finish what you start?"

"All right, my sweet little Ivy vine, you asked for it!"

He bent to grab snow from the ground and packed it, but not too hard. He wasn't out for annihilation. He made a quick stockpile, and when he glanced up again, Ivy had taken her stance behind the car.

"That's wiley of you," he said. "Running to your fort, are you? Can't fight in the open?"

"A girl has to protect herself, you know."

He tossed his entire pile, one right after another, watching a couple of them thud against the car but knowing others came very close to finding their mark. Hers, still too light to be effective, came his way with little success.

Three small children came out of the apartment building opposite, heavily bundled with only their eyes showing. They lined up like little soldiers standing sentinel to watch.

"Hi, kids," Ivy greeted. "Want to play?"

Three little heads bobbed.

"Okay. You're on my team, all right?"

The agreement was instant. The three made their way to Ivy's side in a waddling run.

"So you think you can get me by calling in the troops, huh?" he called. Barely holding his laughter in check, he quickly made another stockpile of medium-size snowballs.

Growing braver, Ivy stepped from behind her car to launch the new offensive. One by one, the three little people stood beside her, all throwing their best. He tossed his own with wide aim, having no intentions of hitting any of the small trio. Ivy laughed in pure glee when one of her snow clumps actually hit him, wetly sliding down his cheek.

"Yoo-hoo...Ivy," faintly came through the air in Arletta's warbling voice. "Telephone..."

Ivy raised her hands signaling a time-out. "Sorry—looks like the game's over," she announced, preparing to depart.

He swiveled, snowball in hand, to follow her back to the apartment.

Immediately, his feet flew out from under him and he landed flat out against the snow piled near the sidewalk.

"Attack," Ivy yelled.

Three little giggling bodies ringed him, pelting him with snow. Kneeling, Ivy simply scooped snow from the ground right over him, joining the childish laughter with her own high merriment.

"I surrender," he cried, looking into Ivy's shining eyes. This was the first they'd ever had of a totally carefree moment, and the exhilaration of it went right to his heart. He wished they could remain snowbound for the entire day. "You got me."

The blue-green in her eyes darkened with his words. Something shifted while he watched. A softness closed up. Her laughter faded to a smile.

"I have to go." She rose from beside him to brush the snow from her knees. "Aunt Arletta is calling me to come in."

"Aw, shucks, Ivy. Can you come out and play later?" he complained in the same way he would've had he been ten. He let his voice dip seductively. "I'll meet you out here and we can build a snow fort."

"I don't think so." She watched the children wander away to play on their own. A fleeting look of longing crossed her face before she said with regret, "There's too much to do."

"Like what?" That was her trouble, Noah suddenly knew. She didn't have enough time to play and was afraid to let herself start. And according to what Aunt Arletta told him, her girlhood had been cut short when her father died. She'd never had a chance to make up for the lost time.

"Like chores and committee work and church."

"After church, then?"

"I'm going out with Gerald."

"Oh, yeah." He tried not to let his disappointment show, knowing that once they left for church all his own direct contact with Ivy would be lost for the day. He would no longer have her to himself. She and Arletta usually sat with friends. He'd become merely another friend in the crowd of worshipers.

She had a long list of calls to make this week, too. He'd seen her to-do calendar, the one that held her work schedule. And the extra numbers to phone in connection with Gerry's project.

A feeling of antipathy for Ivy's involvement settled over his shoulders like a heavy cloak. He struggled to shrug it off; it had nothing to do with him. Not his business. He thought perhaps at the close of the morning church service it would be better for him to hitch a ride from someone besides Ivy to collect his truck from Brookside. He might be tempted to let his anger with Gerry show, and Lord knew he was working on that part of his life. It was something he continued to pray about.

Then next week he planned to fly to California to spend Christmas with his parents. He wasn't likely to see Ivy again until after the holidays. But he didn't tell her that now. He said, merely, "Well, have a good time," and let it go as he followed her inside.

The phone call had been from Kelly. Ivy went into

her bedroom to return it. After a cup of coffee, Noah tromped outside again to finish clearing the car of snow by himself.

"Why don't you put someone else in charge of the store and come with me?" Gerald asked as they strolled the Plaza streets looking into store windows. In spite of the snow, the entire area shone with its traditional Christmas lights. The streets were choked with cars and vans full of gazing families.

Ivy didn't answer. There wasn't a serious tone to his lighthearted request anyway. They'd been talking of what the committee could do while he was gone, but now the conversation had turned to his agenda in Europe over the holiday. She listened to his descriptions of brand-new luxury hotels where he sometimes stayed to conduct business, and of small old-world style inns, town squares and unusual shops and streets which held rich details of a bygone time. It all sounded so wonderful and exciting.

At the moment, Ivy doubted she'd ever see any of it. Not the way her life was now. And Gerry certainly didn't understand a thing about being in business for oneself if he could suggest she blithely hand over the reins to another during her busiest time of year.

Gerry moved closer, taking her arm, their path narrowed by the piles of snow on each side. Her mind drifted for a moment to all the things on her to-do list. Fortunately, Brad had agreed to clean the sidewalk in front of Wall's Intrigue by morning and she didn't have to worry about doing it herself.

"Well?" Gerry prompted.

She chuckled, flashing a teasing glance back at him. "Oh, sure, just like that! You are a dreamer."

"Why not?" His smile edged up, his blue eyes taking on a deeper glow. "You deserve a break. You've never been to Europe. You'd love it."

"I'm sure I would, Gerry, but I can't just walk away from my responsibilities like that." They passed another couple exiting a restaurant. "I own a small business, remember? Besides, my cash flow wouldn't cover a trip to Europe."

"Ways can always be found, Ivy, if you want to come."

She glanced sideways at him, trying to assess how seriously he meant his suggestion. Something in his gaze told her he was very serious. Her heart beat a little faster as she considered it very carefully. She was afraid to ask if he meant that as an invitation to travel at his expense. Or as his girlfriend, with all that term entailed and implied in today's modern terms?

Maybe that was why none of her relationships ever worked. She'd never been willing to go that direction of modern thinking and attitudes; her faith in the Bible teachings meant more to her than mere lip service. Yet she knew she was no different than other women. She desperately wanted to love and be loved. She just wanted it to be in the bounds of marriage.

Across the street, a small crowd gathered around a performing group of singers. Ivy slowed her steps, listening to the words of "Oh Little Town of Bethlehem." They reminded her she'd skipped an evening Christmas concert at church to share this time with Gerry.

Ivy loved the old songs and was always deeply moved by their telling of a Savior born. She thought of all the times she needed to hear that, needed the heart-lifting knowledge of her own salvation.

In her best daydreams, a trip to Europe would be among the top five picks of things to do, and going with Gerry would be a whale of good time. But as much as she felt tempted...

"I can't leave my aunt," she finally murmured.

"Hmm... Perhaps one day." He changed the subject abruptly, hailing a horse-drawn open carriage. "Let's take a carriage ride. This is the perfect night for it."

And it was a perfect ride, snuggled against Gerry's side, the loveliest ending to a date she'd had in ages. Never mind her comparing blue eyes with warm brown ones.

Monday dawned with a bright winter sun reflecting off everything. Ivy flipped her sun visor down, squinting to prevent too much light from blinding her as she drove the few miles to Wall's Intrigue at seven. Counters she had neglected to straighten Saturday night needed attention and she had to unpack more merchandise. The Brookside merchants had invested in a joint newspaper ad in the Sunday paper; she seriously doubted the piles of snow would keep too many customers home today. Not with it being the last ten days before Christmas. From experience, she knew her next week and a half would demand sixteen-hour days and every ounce of her energy.

Her premise of sixteen-hour days proved to be true. Ivy kept Sherri almost as busy as herself, begged Brad for all his extra time, and cajoled and arranged baby-sitting for Emily. Making phone calls early and late, she kept the Deborah's Dwelling committee up-to-date on the project's progress right up until three days before Christmas, when they'd all agreed to rest it until after the holidays.

Too busy to miss anyone, a whole week sailed by before she realized she hadn't heard from Noah since their romp in the snow. Aunt Arletta hadn't mentioned him, either.

Barbara called one day asking for Matt's phone number and seemed greatly disappointed when Sherri couldn't give it to her. Ivy let out a sigh of relief, because she'd promised Matt to keep the number in the strictest confidence.

It did give her a reason to call Matt, though. And in calling Matt, she learned Noah had left early that morning to visit his parents. Perhaps he'd told Aunt Arletta, but he hadn't bothered to tell her. He hadn't taken the time to call and say goodbye.

But then, why should he? She wasn't his keeper. They were merely friends. And she'd heard from Gerry a couple of times since he'd been out of town. He'd called twice to speak about the committee progress, quickly turning that to personal exchange. He also sent her a dozen roses along with a lovely note mentioning how nice he thought their carriage ride had been, saying they should do it again sometime.

"Oh, yes, didn't I mention it?" her aunt said that evening as Ivy fell exhausted into bed. "Noah told me ages ago that he'd be away over the holidays. And Matt and little Chad are with Chad's aunt. Shirley will be with her sister, I think. It looks like our Christmas table will have only us around it this year, Ivy dear."

Ivy nodded. That was fine. A day of solitude wouldn't do her any harm. Usually by Christmas she enjoyed the day better when it was quiet. She needed the rest. And she and Aunt Arletta could always contemplate the day with reverence instead of boisterous activity. Almost all the snow from ten days back was gone, so they might even enjoy a leisurely stroll in the afternoon.

There was just no accounting for her let-down feelings.

Chapter Fourteen

Ivy drove home Christmas eve with gifts for Aunt Arletta, tired but well satisfied. Satisfied, that is, with her store. Her season's income was the highest in Wall's Intrigue history. She'd given Sherri a real bonus for the first time, and a deep discount to Emily, who'd used the opportunity to buy several gifts. Brad had been thrilled with something a little extra in his paycheck, too, and promised to deliver an envelope to Matt and Chad.

In spite of those euphoric feelings, a small core of loneliness crept over her. She tried to push it away. She wasn't alone—never alone when she had the Lord with her and Aunt Arletta. And friends like Kelly and Scott and...

She hadn't heard from either Noah or Gerry for days.

Well, never mind. Count your blessings, Aunt A had taught her. Yes, that was the thing to do—count a new blessing with each block she drove. She began.

She'd talked with her mother by phone this morning. Mom was happy as a lark down in Phoenix, loved the warmer climate, and her husband, Richard, was teaching her to play golf.

And Ivy was so very glad she had Aunt Arletta to greet her at home. Her apartment was seldom empty or dark.

Kelly and Scott, affectionate and always offering something new in fun and worthwhile projects to fill her leisure time—what little of it she had. But Ivy realized Kelly no longer needed or depended on her friendship as she once had; she had Scott.

It seemed Ivy was destined to spend another Christmas without either husband or children. That goal had been kicked over to her ten-year plan for sure. Maybe out of her life plan altogether? Was this how it would always be from Christmas to Christmas, year to year? Would she become another of the over thirty, then over forty crowd at church looking to friendship to fill those gaps?

She didn't or couldn't discount that bunch—their friendship and honest caring had stood the test of time with each other, and they would be there for her if she only reached out. It was just that she wanted a husband of her own, a loving relationship in marriage. Like her mom and her dad had enjoyed. Like Kelly and Scott.

Well, never mind, she told herself again. She had her store…

That was another matter on her mind. Today she'd learned that a larger space a few doors away would come open in about three months. Dreams of taking it danced in her head like the proverbial sugar plums. But it was scary. More space, but more rent and running expenses. Should she bid for it? Should she risk expanding so quickly? Was her timing right?

She wished she had someone with whom she could discuss it. She probably could find someone at the small business association to which she belonged to toss around ideas with, but that wasn't right now, tonight.

At a red light, she sighed and stretched her arms in front of her to relieve some of the exhaustion. Even counting her blessings and thinking about her business possibilities, she still felt a little flat. The long hours had caught up to her, she suspected. A good sleep and a restful day tomorrow would set her right.

Aunt Arletta, wearing a softly knitted pumpkin-orange sweater and matching beret, handed her a cup of hot chocolate as soon as she walked through the door and peeled out of her coat.

"I figured you might need a refresher, Ivy."

"You're dressed," Ivy said, kicking off her shoes.

"Well, of course."

"Um...?" Ivy sipped her cocoa, walking toward her bedroom.

"I thought we could go to the midnight service, dear. Kelly called and said she and Scott were planning to be there. I just knew you'd want to go, too, so I told her to expect us."

Ivy tried not to let her shoulders slump. All she wanted was a hot shower and to fall into bed. The Lord knew she had no energy left. Taking a deep breath, she turned and attempted a cheery smile. Her aunt's face carried a soft expectation.

"The midnight Christmas service?"

It was the first of its kind for their church and

Ivy'd totally forgotten about it. She couldn't bear to disappoint Aunt A. The poor dear had barely been out of the apartment all week. Ivy had had no time to take her around.

You've had little time for me, either, Ivy. Come. Come to me and I will give you rest...

Suddenly, a deep desire to attend the service assailed her, filling her with a need so strong it could not be denied. Her life had been so hectic these past few months she felt as if her spirit had been sadly neglected. Her relationship with the Lord had been slighted, she admitted, and she longed to commune with Him. It was just the thing to put her into the true spirit of Christmas.

"Okay, Aunt Arletta. Let me just put my feet up for thirty minutes. I have time for that, don't I?"

Later, they quietly entered the church just as the lone guitarist began a soft strumming accompaniment to "Silent Night." Ivy could have sung it in her sleep, and she knew Aunt Arletta could, too. When she lifted her voice to join, Kelly turned in the pew just in front of her to give her a sweet smile of welcome.

She returned it, already glad she'd come.

Their youngest pastor, John Daniels, opened his Bible but then spoke from memory, his voice full of quiet emotion. Listening to the old story told thousands of times this very night, Ivy closed her eyes. Would it ever grow tiresome?

Lord, I am frazzled to the bone, but hearing the glad news that gives us Christmas fills me with renewed strength and a deep, deep well of happiness. I know you will lead me to the right answers about whether or not to increase the business at this time.

And with you to fill my heart, how can I feel lonely? Thank you, Lord, for Aunt Arletta, and for blessing my business year and I'll go on trusting in you about...well...you know. This coming year? Maybe this is the year when I'll find him, the man I've waited for?

A drifting image of soft brown eyes imposed itself over her dialogue with the Lord. She tried to push it away, tried to get back her concentration, but Noah's smile, the way his lips curved into his cheeks joined the thoughts of the way his eyes shone when he'd thrown snowballs at her. Or teased her. Or kissed her.

She remembered their Thanksgiving kiss altogether too often.

Why hadn't Gerry kissed her? Or teased her?

Gerry wasn't the teasing kind, she remembered in defensive reaction. And Gerry had sent her roses....

But both men had gone elsewhere to celebrate Christmas.

She sighed, eyeing the couples in the congregation, teenagers to grandparents. They made up more than half the worshipers. When would she ever be important enough in a man's eyes to be first in his consideration? When would she have a marriage partner who reached for her hand when a loving prayer was given?

The service closed on a soft, sweet note of reverence, yet the joy of the season permeated the departing worshipers. Ivy exchanged greetings and hugs with Kelly and Scott and other good friends. Across the aisle, Aunt Arletta made her own rounds, making Ivy smile. Aunt A gave out so many murmured "God bless yous" that she rivaled John Daniels.

Some people had no family at all.

Thank you, Lord, for reminding me how very blessed I am…I won't ask for more right now.

She wouldn't worry about anything for the next few days, she decided. Not business, not Gerry, not Noah.

Especially not Noah.

The next morning, after she and Aunt Arletta exchanged gifts, she found a stray package under her tree, unmarked except with her name. She glanced a question toward her aunt, who only shrugged.

"Don't ask me, Ivy. I didn't put it there."

"Well, how did it get here?"

"I've no idea. Why don't you unwrap it?"

Ivy hadn't felt as excited by a gift since her dad died. With a leaping heart she carefully opened the soft gold paper.

It was a small gold ring with a pearl cluster in a heart mount. Ivy simply stared at it, murmuring in awed pleasure.

"Oh, my…it's lovely. But Aunt A, who would give me a ring?" A ring was a personal gift, a promise of friendship or love.

At sixteen, she hadn't even expected one from Eric. Dan had given her a ring with a tiny diamond. She'd gushed at how romantic it made her feel…and sadly returned it after their breakup.

The engagement ring from Leon had held diamonds all right. Big diamonds in a splashy setting worth a hefty sum. Thrilled to own something so beautiful, she also was a little embarrassed over his obvious display. Funny how she could now laugh over his angry, self-centered demand for it back.

This ring wasn't intended as an engagement ring,

Ivy suspected. It was meant to honor friendship. But who was the giver?

Too small to fit her ring finger, she slipped it on the little finger of her right hand, then held her hand to the light to inspect its effect. It made her fingers look longer, her hand more graceful.

She picked up the box and checked the signature stamp of a well-known jeweler. The ring came from a fine store.

It must be Gerry. It could only be from Gerry because Ivy couldn't think of another person of her acquaintance who would pick out something so elegant. It was a little early in their growing relationship, Ivy mused, but it was the kind of gift she'd expect from him. The gift held a world of promise.

It must be a sign from the Lord, too. Hadn't she prayed only last night again for a husband to come within her sights? She'd waited a long time for the perfect groom.

She sighed with renewed hope.

By New Year's Eve day, traffic had dropped off considerably at Wall's Intrigue. Ivy let Sherri go home at one and worked on schedules for January. She'd set an inventory date and brought the first half of her computer file of suppliers up to par, but her plans for Reeves House began to take precedence on her timetable.

She had no idea when Gerry would return. Barbara said she'd had a quick phone call from him just yesterday, but his only message to Ivy had been to carry on with the Deborah's Dwelling plans and if she had to measure anything for Reeves House to simply phone ahead to the Marshalls to let her into the house.

She and Barbara had plans for next week to get the invitations in the mail to the Valentine's Dance benefit. Ivy still felt a little staggered at all the city's leading names on the list.

Ivy put down her pen and rubbed her temples. The rest of it could wait until another day. She wanted to go home.

She locked the front door at four, turning the sign to Closed. She gazed from her front window a moment with only her night-lights aglow against the growing dusk. On the street, restaurant lights looked softly inviting, the laughter of strollers and party goers brighter, gaiety for the New Years celebration already in the air.

New Year's Eve. It seemed all the world wanted to recognize a new year. A new beginning?

She turned away, donned her jacket, exited her back door and locked it…then heard her phone ring. But she let it go. If someone really needed her, they'd call her apartment.

Kelly had invited her to attend a concert with her and Scott and there had been other invitations for the evening, but she wasn't in the mood for any of it. Besides, she really didn't want to leave Aunt Arletta alone. For once, Shirley wasn't available.

A quiet evening at home would make up for the one she didn't get on Christmas Eve, Ivy mused. And she was due one. She and Aunt Arletta could play dominoes, Aunt A's favorite game.

It would be just the thing. Or so she thought…

The smell of popcorn met her at the door.

A low velvety murmur fell silent from the kitchen,

sending all her senses on alert. Had she heard what she thought she had? She hadn't seen Noah's truck in the parking lot.

Then a rattle of dice, a little boy's squeal.

"Not fair!" A sophisticated female tone raised a protest.

"It's perfectly fair," Matt replied without compunction. Ivy had rarely—if ever—heard his voice sound so confident, so relaxed. "You landed on my space. You owe me four hundred and fifty dollars. Pay up."

"Daddy plays tough," Chad consoled.

"He certainly does," Noah said. "He's a tough character."

"Well, I haven't any more money," Barbara announced. "Put it on my credit card."

"That's the trouble with you women," came Matt's teasing grumble. "You think credit cards solve everything."

"When is Ivy supposed to be home?" Barbara asked.

"As a matter of fact, I thought I heard the door a moment ago," Aunt Arletta replied. "She promised to be home early."

"And so I am," Ivy said, entering the kitchen. She let her gaze travel the circle, taking in the board game vying for space with bowls of popcorn, peanuts and snack crackers. "What's all this?"

"Nothing much, Ivy." Noah's irrepressible grin flashed her way while his gaze made a slow pass over her surprised expression. "Aunt Arletta thought a small party would be fun when I called this morning. Spontaneous!"

"Uh-huh." She should've taken time to refresh

her makeup before leaving the store, she fumed. Why she should care, she couldn't imagine, when Noah had often seen her with none at all. "Why didn't you call, Aunt A?"

"Oh, I meant to, Ivy. But you did say this morning that you wanted to stay in tonight and you'd be home early."

"Well, yeah."

"Surprised you, huh?" Noah's dark eyes sparkled.

"I don't mind surprises, I suppose. I guess if I did..."

"She wouldn't like living with me, would you, Ivy?" Her aunt finished Ivy's thought as she filled up glasses with her own lemonade mix. "We'll have a quiet good time and enjoy the New Year with no stress or strain."

Ivy greeted the other guests and, though she now recalled seeing Matthew's van in the parking lot, wondered how she'd missed spotting Barbara's bright red sports car.

"Your aunt very kindly included me in her invitation," Barbara said. "We just started this game. Want to join?"

"No, I'd rather just watch this round. Ah, Barb, I thought you were going to a fancy gathering somewhere?"

"Oh," Barbara glanced quickly toward Matt before riveting her attention on little red houses on the board in front of her. "Well, the Singleton parties are all alike. Been to one, seen them all. They won't miss me. Besides, Chad's more fun. Aren't you, scout?"

The little boy sat between Barbara and his father, the telephone book and a cushion raising his height.

"Uh-huh. It's funner when Aunt Arletta sings, too. She sings really silly songs." Chad gazed at Barbara with large solemn eyes. "Why do you call me scout?"

"Oh, it's just a phrase." Barbara waved her hand airily.

"Go change your clothes, Ivy. Jeans or sweats," Noah directed, rolling the dice. "No one's dressed up at this party."

She shot him an irritated glance. "I can see that, thank you."

"Must've been a long week," he returned with a grin, jumping his game piece. "Our little Ivy vine is growing snappy."

"Your week must've had nothing in it at all to have grown so lazy out in sunny California."

"Ouch. You wound me, sweet Ivy." He thumped his chest. "Right here. Did you miss me that much?"

"Cried into my pillow, every night."

"You did? That bad?"

Opening her mouth for another retort, Ivy became aware all at once of four pairs of very observant eyes. Even Chad's gaze was agog with interest. She pursed her mouth instead.

"I think it's teatime," Noah said, a bit of smugness in his tone. "A hot cup of tea will soothe your ragged edges, Ivy."

"I'm going to change." Turning on her heel, she headed toward her bedroom, wanting to stomp but holding in that childish gesture with an iron will. She wouldn't give Noah the satisfaction. Or the others anything to speculate over.

"I'll make it, Aunt A," she heard Noah say. "You

sit and enjoy the game. Have to make myself useful or I might grow lazy."

Ivy ignored that one. Three steps into the hall, she asked her usual question. "Any messages, Aunt A?"

"Um, a couple. Haley and Kelly, I think. And Gerry."

That stopped her. She returned to the kitchen door. "Gerry?"

"Mmm..."

Ivy glanced at Barbara. "I didn't realize he was home. When did he call, Aunt A?"

"He came in late last night, I think," Barbara remarked, concentrating on helping Chad play the game.

"Oh, about an hour ago, I suppose," Aunt Arletta responded. "I told him to try you at the store, but he said no one answered. He left a message earlier."

The phone call she'd let go. What had he wanted? Was he eager to see her after two weeks away? Or did he merely want to confirm their dates for work on Reeves House?

She fingered her ring.

"I expect he wants to check on the plans for next week. I'll just go return a call and find out."

Ivy closed the bedroom door behind her. Turning on her answering machine, she turned the volume down. She shed her blouse and skirt while listening to first Kelly and then Haley, but then she threw herself down on her bed when Gerry's voice came on.

"Hi, Ivy. Listen, I know I'm a jerk to call at the last minute, but I'm home earlier than I anticipated, and here's the thing. I've several parties to go to, and I'd like to take you with me. Anyway, it's about, oh, one or thereabout now. Give me a ring by four if you can come, all right? Tried the shop. Couldn't get you."

One? Where had she been at one?

She'd slipped out of the store for a quick sandwich just before letting Sherri go home. But Sherri hadn't given her a message.

Swiftly punching in Gerry's number, she let it ring until his machine switched on. "Hi Gerry, returning your call. Sorry to have missed you. Have a good evening."

There was nothing more she could do. She tried not to let her disappointment rule. Trading a last-minute opportunity of a glamorous evening for the one waiting for her in the kitchen wasn't a real option anyway. She could never bring herself to be so rude.

If only Gerry had called her yesterday. She pushed the let-down emotions aside. Gerry had said his early return was unexpected.

Laughter from the other end of the apartment burst out. Above the others, she heard Noah's deep chuckle. Despite herself, the sound rippled all through her like a favorite song.

Noah was back, too. Suddenly she didn't really mind missing an evening with Gerry. She could totally be herself with the kitchen crowd. It promised to be a relaxing evening after all.

Sometime after midnight, after apple cider toasts and hearty good wishes along with sincere prayers for a happy new year, the company said good-night.

"I'll see everyone out, Aunt Arletta," Ivy said, observing her aunt's droopy eyelids as coats and hats were gathered. "And don't you dare try to clean up until late tomorrow morning. I'll be up by then and we'll tackle it together."

"All right, Ivy. I'll abide with that."

"Thanks, Aunt A, for inviting me to come this evening," Barbara murmured almost shyly. She cast a swift glance toward Matt. "I can't remember when I've had so much fun and good company."

"Thank Noah, too," Aunt Arletta muttered past her hand covering a yawn. "It was his—"

"We had a great time, Aunt Arletta," Noah interjected. "We should do this more often."

Barbara and Matt were already out the door before Noah gathered a sleeping Chad from the living room couch onto his shoulder. Behind him, Ivy switched off lights, leaving the Christmas tree lights to glow for one last hurrah before being packed away for another year.

Noah hesitated at the half-opened door as though he wanted to say one last good-night. His gaze roved her face in the near darkness, a lingering tenderness shimmered in the dark depths of his eyes.

"I'll come along about midmorning myself, Ivy, to help clean up. Don't you do anything more tonight, either, you hear?. Sleep late in the morning. But we should plan to clear out the holiday decorations from the law offices on Saturday night, don't you think?"

"Oh! Yes, of course. Shears and Watson. It's a date."

Now why had she gone and said it that way? It wasn't a date! No date. It was a business arrangement, that was all. "Um..."

"Don't worry about it, sweet Ivy vine." He touched the tip of her nose with one finger, then as swiftly as the midnight moment, while holding Chad firmly, bent and kissed her. His lips held a sweetness she longed to capture, a feeling of inexplicable treasure. But then the warm sensation was gone again so quickly, she wondered if her imagination had run riot with heady New Year's celebration.

"We'll work it out tomorrow," he murmured.

She could only nod.

Chapter Fifteen

Ivy looked both groggy and surprised when Noah knocked on her door about ten. He eyed the huge white man's shirt she wore over a Christmas print T-shirt.

He didn't know why, but the sight of her wearing a man's shirt shot yearning for her up his spine as nothing else had. But he suddenly knew he didn't want her wearing any man's clothing but his own. His. Someday after they were married.

He wasn't in a position yet to ask her. He wasn't at all sure she'd say yes when he did.

"I didn't really think you'd show," she confessed past a huge yawn.

"Didn't you sleep well?" he asked her.

"Well, when I could sleep," she mumbled, ruffling her hair.

Several unruly curls bounced near her cheekbone. Fascinated, he had a deep urge to flick one just to see it bounce again, to smooth it between his fingers. One day, he promised himself.

"The party next door broke up about two, I think," she continued. "Then later someone roared by on a loud motorbike."

"I slept the sleep of the just and didn't hear a thing," Aunt Arletta remarked, loading dishes into the dishwasher. "But I just may take a nap this afternoon, anyway."

"Well, I bunked out on Matt's couch for a change," he said, tossing his coat on the sofa. He had to change the direction of his stare or Ivy might get the idea he was there just to see her two days in a row. Or repeat last night's kiss.

A wise man knew when to play it cool, he reminded himself.

"His neighborhood was quiet. And I promised Chad I'd take him to the park this afternoon, so let's get this cleanup going."

Grabbing a broom from the corner mop closet, he set about sweeping the kitchen floor with vigor, noting but ignoring the doubtful look Ivy threw him.

"Really, Noah. You don't have to—"

"Nope." He caught three popcorn pieces in his broom and brushed them into a pile. "No objections, now. We helped make the mess while enjoying your hospitality, Ivy. I can help clean up."

"Well, in that case, you can help move the couch and chairs in the living room so I can vacuum under them. And as long as you're offering, you can stick around long enough to haul the tree out, if you please. I've already taken all the decorations off and—"

"All right, all right. I got the picture. You've just been waiting for a little muscle power around here, admit it. You did miss me while I was gone, didn't you?''

''Hah! Don't think that just because you've become a fixture around here that we can't get along without you.''

That's what worried him, he guessed. So far he hadn't made himself indispensable to Ivy, although he'd tried. Trouble was she'd already gotten along without him for twenty-seven years, and he didn't see anything in her attitude that showed him she needed him, or wanted him any more now than she had weeks ago.

Lord, I know she's the right woman for me...when is she going to notice I'm the right man for her?

He'd noticed how quickly she'd gone to her bedroom to return Gerry's call last night. But he still maintained that Gerry wasn't the man for her. He'd just have to hold his own until she recognized it.

But he prayed he was right. Every day. So far he hadn't heard the Lord tell him anything different. He told himself he had to trust Ivy to make the right choice. And he had to be patient.

He heard the vacuum turn on in the next room. He tossed a grin toward Aunt Arletta and went to help Ivy. Without a word between them, he lifted the couch and moved the chairs around while she vacuumed. Then getting a garbage bag from the kitchen, he stuffed in the small tree, now totally bare, and set off to haul it outside.

Thinking it would take him only a minute, he left his coat behind and started down the sidewalk at a fast clip. But before he could reach the trash bins, he saw Shirley standing in her open doorway. Something about her distracted expression gave him pause.

Underneath her robe, her feet were bare. Her fingers twisted together so tightly her knucklebones stuck out.

"Shirley?" he murmured. "Is something wrong?"

Her mouth trembled. Her faded blue eyes pooled. For a moment he wasn't sure she recognized him. "I need..."

"Shirley, do you need assistance?"

"Yes, please, Noah. I..." Shivering with cold, her eyes pleaded for help.

"Here," he set his garbage bag down and took her elbow as he stepped through her door, closing it behind him. "Let me help you sit down a moment."

Not sure if he should leave her, he guided her to a chair. He squatted before her, trying to read her face, wishing he had more medical experience to tell him if she was in the midst of a crisis or not. But he thought her distress more emotional than a medical need. "Now tell me what's wrong? Are you ill?"

Shirley shook her head. "My daughter needs me..." A tear rolled down her cheek.

"Where is she?"

Not answering, she continued to cry softly. Murmuring for her to wait where she was, he left her and raced the few yards back to Ivy's, shoving urgently through the door.

"Why, Noah, what—?" Arletta looked up in surprise.

"Aunt A, please come down to Shirley's. Something's wrong and I think she needs you."

A sober gaze settled over her features. "Be right there, Noah, as soon as I get my shoes on."

He waited just inside the door feeling helpless, looking beyond the courtyard to the parking lot, listening to Arletta's murmur to Ivy from the bedroom area. When she reappeared, he took Arletta's elbow and they hurried along to Shirley's apartment.

"Shirley, dear, what's wrong?" Arletta demanded as soon as they stepped up to the door.

"I need to go to Candy."

"I thought that's where you were, dear."

"No. That husband of hers didn't want me around. I came home last night."

"Well, what's happened now?"

"The boys called. They…that man… Oh, Arletta, she's hurt!"

"How, Shirley? How is she hurt? Was there an accident?"

"No. No accident. Not this time. Not last time, either. Her husband hit her, then took her car and left." The tears ran freely down her face with her plaintive cry. "I have to go get her, Arletta, she's scared, and the boys are scared, but I can't get a taxi. Can you and Ivy drive me there? Or Noah?"

"I'll see about Ivy's car," he muttered, feeling the older woman's desperation. He'd faced emergencies a time or two but he'd never seen a case of domestic abuse or its ugly outreach firsthand. He wasn't sure what to do.

"Yes, do that, Noah," Arletta instructed, her eyes sharp and purposeful. "Meanwhile, Shirley and I will dress and meet you and Ivy in the parking lot. Now Shirley, put something warm on…"

Noah raced back to the other apartment. "Ivy!"

She came out of the hall, dust cloth in hand. She smiled at him, her eyes alight with teasing. "You left some stuff from your pockets on the lamp table last night. What is this, your vote for another board game?'' She handed him three little red plastic houses amid a couple of folded papers. Her glance fell briefly on them, a slight frown of puzzlement beginning as he closed his fingers around the objects. Almost, he thought, she'd caught the printed logo of the jewelry store where he'd shopped.

He didn't like having to spoil her good mood, but the need to redirect her attention came at a good time.

''Sorry, Ivy, but we need your car keys.''

''Oh?''

''Shirley has to see about her daughter.''

''Is she ill?'' Then with a glance at him, her smile faded. ''Oh.''

He explained what had occurred. ''I gather this is not the first time?''

Ivy shook her head. ''I suppose Aunt Arletta wants to take Shirley over to see her? That's what usually happens.''

''Shirley's pretty upset.''

''Yes, I'm sure she is, and that situation seems to be growing worse. If only Candy would press charges or leave.'' Ivy's helpless anger flared in her eyes a moment before she turned to view the street. ''Well, of course we must take her. I'll see to her, Noah. You've promised Chad...''

''I think I should go along. I'll follow along in the truck.''

''All right. I wonder if Candy needs to go to the hospital emergency room?''

''Don't know.''

''Well, have Aunt A call and find out while I gather coats and purses and such,'' Ivy directed.

After that the day turned long with all of their

sudden involvement in another family's needs. Arletta stayed with the boys while Noah and Ivy drove Shirley and her daughter to the emergency room. They waited patiently for over three hours until Candy could be examined. She had a bruise on her cheek, but was otherwise all right. Then they drove the two back to pack up the boys and Candy after a counselor insisted she spend some time away from the house.

By the time they returned home, it was almost three. Arletta elected to stay to help Shirley with the boys while Candy rested. Noah walked Ivy the two doors down to her own apartment.

"Well, I hate to run away after all this, Ivy, and leave you with the place still in a mess, but I really must."

"Yeah, I know. It's all right," she said with a sigh. She seemed filled with a sad moodiness that set her at a distance, and her thanks were those of a casual acquaintance. "You helped a lot, Noah, thanks. And not with only the housework. I'm sure when Shirley has a chance she'll thank you herself. Tell Chad hello for me, will you please?"

"Sure will, Ivy. I'll pick up Brad for Saturday night. Maybe I'll find someone else to help us pack things up as well. To get it all down faster than it went up."

"That would be great. Thanks again."

Noah's feet dragged as he approached his truck. Leaving Ivy on such a dispirited note was the last thing he wanted to do, but he'd promised Chad. He felt strongly about keeping promises. Especially to a lonely little boy. He'd never break his word unless prevented by a cataclysmic event.

He only wished Ivy knew that. Something deep inside him wanted to assure her that most men weren't like Candy's husband, breaking their word to love and cherish their partners. He'd never understood the insecurities that drove that kind of behavior, but he felt like apologizing for all the men who failed to keep their sacred promises. It wasn't in his makeup, nor Scott's, nor Matt's, nor any of the Christian men he knew personally, but…

The thought struck him that Ivy had suffered her own great disappointments in men. Aunt Arletta had filled in a few details just before Christmas; he hadn't taken the three engagements too seriously, he supposed, because Aunt A had said he shouldn't be concerned. Ivy had been young and searching when those relationships had occurred. But what if he'd underestimated Ivy's hurt over those near disasters, or the distrust they'd left behind?

All at once, he knew what he struggled against, knew how to pray. For Ivy and for himself.

Father, please wash away Ivy's natural distrust of giving too much of herself. Lift her spirit with Yours and fill her heart with Your love. Please help her to see mine, and to understand the deep devotion I want to give her. Teach me patience, Father. Wipe the fear of true loving and loving true from her heart….

On the sixth of January, Ivy rented a van for a week to haul her supplies and small furnishings back and forth to Reeves House. The job had grown from the original request of refurbishing the third-floor hall and ideas on the bedrooms to overseeing the entire upper floor redecorating. Over the discussions with Barbara and Gerry, she'd suggested they open the dark upper rooms with more windows, or even skylights to make them more comfortable and desirable. Intrigued with the idea, Barbara approved the plan immediately. She was especially taken with the idea of opening up the large east end of the attic for a game-video room.

Gerry'd asked Ivy to find a good contractor to do the job. It wasn't the kind of work usually taken on in winter, but after a great deal of searching and with good recommendations, she'd found a reputable builder. Weather permitting, they'd begin tomorrow.

"I'll call you periodically to see how things are going," she told Sherri as she climbed into the dark-blue van. She'd gone over last-minute instructions twice, feeling a bit foolish at her nervous excitement but unable to put it aside.

The enormity of her first big project had her checking details down to the tiniest need. She'd chosen the look she wanted with care, one that she felt would serve Reeves House well. Gerry's and Barbara's approval of her sketches made her lightheaded with delight; her reputation as an interior designer could grow enormously if she did a good job for them. She wanted to give it her very best effort.

She looked at the heavy gray sky. Thank goodness, only the contractor would be there today; the actual work should start tomorrow when the weatherman promised a sunny day.

"Lord, I know it's January, but you often send us a thaw about now. I would count it a blessing for one to grace us for a week or so. Please let the work run smoothly and in a reasonable time frame. And oh, yes. Help me to regain my cool at home."

She'd left the house totally out of sorts with Aunt

Arletta. Her aunt had given away her favorite sweater.

In fact she hadn't missed it until this morning when she went searching through her bottom drawer. It was the perfect thing to wear over her jeans to Reeves House this morning, she mused, pretty but work-hearty.

"Aunt A," she'd called, replacing the clothing she'd taken out to make sure she hadn't missed it. "Have you seen my turquoise lamb's-wool sweater?"

From the kitchen, she heard a mumble. Ivy raised her head at the cautious tone. Getting up from the floor, she went to tackle the subject. "Aunt Arletta?"

"Well, Ivy, you know the clothing drive the young people from church have going..." Aunt Arletta's blue eyes gazed at her with all innocence and defensive goodwill.

"You didn't."

"But Ivy, they really needed more things," Aunt Arletta said, spreading her hands. "They had lots of children's outgrown clothing this year, but not much good women's clothes, and that sweet little Jones girl fell in love with it right off."

"So did I when I bought it, Aunt Arletta, and I wasn't through wearing it yet." Her jaw went hard. "Why didn't you check with me first?"

"I tried, Ivy, but you were busy. That sweater is at least three years old and you haven't worn it once this year. I thought you didn't like it anymore."

She couldn't fault Aunt Arletta for good observation, Ivy fumed. "Well, I wanted to wear it this morning," she grumped. "What else did you give away?"

"Nothing that would interest you, dear."

"You know my closet is strictly off-limits. You haven't—?"

"I didn't touch anything in your closet, Ivy, I assure you." Aunt Arletta's eyes clouded with hurt. "Although, in my opinion, there are things in there that should be passed along to people who could use them. Seems to me with all your fussing about never enough storage space you'd want to clear out certain things. Why hold on to anything that just takes up space but serves no earthly good, I'd like to know? Or heavenly, either?"

Ivy had no answer to that, but her irritation refused to soften.

Her aunt meant well. She always did. But her enthusiasm to help others carried her too far at times. Like with the young people at church and their clothes closet drive. It was an annual gathering of extra clothing for those in need and always created havoc in their household. Three years ago, Ivy had outright forbidden her aunt to touch anything in her closet. Anything at all.

Her own fault lay in forgetting to mention her drawer chest was off-limits as well, Ivy reminded herself now as she turned into the long drive that led to Reeves House. She should've known better than to leave their contribution to Aunt Arletta alone. Last year, Ivy'd taken the time to sort through her own things for the clothing drive and contributed money besides. This year, the effort had simply slipped past her.

But she did wonder, as it suddenly struck her as funny, how she'd kept all those wedding and bridesmaids dresses in the back of her closet from Aunt

A's invasion all this time. Those were the things Aunt A wanted her to give away.

Ivy sighed. Why she'd kept them only the Lord knew, but Aunt A was right. It was time to clear it all out. She honestly didn't care if she never looked at any of those dresses again; they no longer meant anything to her, especially not defeat.

Was that why she'd hung on to them? To remind herself of the hurt they represented?

Lord, help me, I don't want to live there. I refuse to dwell in defeat—that's why I have my five- and ten-year plans. Please, Father, give me wisdom about my own failings—and where I can move on in my life.

She took a deep cleansing breath of release. Since Christmas eve, it seemed she sometimes looked at things in a new light. And hadn't the Lord promised her a new year?

Still, cleaning out her closet would involve time she didn't have.

If she was very careful how she worded her request, could she trust Aunt Arletta to do it for her? That thought made her chuckle aloud. Her aunt would think she'd gained a plum of a job and it would go a long way toward soothing Aunt A's ruffled feelings.

She called her just as soon as she reached the mansion drive, leaving her aunt on a high note.

The building contractor waited for her as she pulled up to the front door. Mrs. Marshall silently let them in and led them upstairs, where Mr. Marshall was engaged in moving all the bedroom furniture into one room, then he disappeared as silently.

Gerry came up while they pored over the sketches,

discussing various points of change. The builder left, promising his crew would be on the spot by eight the next morning.

"Now that the project has begun, Ivy, how about coming downstairs for some coffee?" Gerry said. "We could go over these lists for Deborah's Dwelling."

"I have an idea," she countered, throwing him a coaxing smile. She wasn't too sure Gerry had ever participated in anything so mundane as physical work. "Why don't you give me a hand with this wallpaper? Many hands make light work, you know, and you'll have fun knowing you did some of it. And the faster we get started, the quicker the project will be complete."

"Oh, um, okay. But only if you promise to come down later."

"It's a deal."

Chapter Sixteen

"Ivy." Aunt Arletta's voice came over the phone without preliminary chitchat. It was about 10:00 a.m. a couple of days later, and Ivy was preparing to leave the store. She was already thirty minutes behind, and glanced at her watch as if she could make it slow down. "I told Candy to come see you about a job this morning. I told her it wouldn't pay much, but it's a new place for her to start. Can you talk with her?'

"Aunt Arletta," Ivy said as she shifted the receiver to rest between her shoulder and her ear while she reached for her purse. The new curtain and drape swatches that had come in just yesterday sat in stacks beside her, ready to go. Barbara had casually mentioned that her bedroom could do with a makeover, and as long as Ivy was coming out to oversee the various work crews, she might just as well have them include her room.

"I'm going to be out to Reeves House for the rest of the day. I explained last night—"

"Oh, of course you did, Ivy. I simply forgot. Well, what about this evening when you get home?"

"Aunt Arletta..." she said on a sighing protest. Since the holiday season was over and Emily had consented to stay on, Ivy really didn't need another clerk just at this time. This pinch would last only a few weeks. Besides that, she preferred to take care of business in the store herself.

"Please, Ivy. Or maybe someone else on the street?"

Uh-oh. Ivy knew what that meant. If Ivy couldn't find a job for Candy, Aunt Arletta wasn't above pestering one of the other businesses to give her latest cause a break. Ivy was certain she didn't want Aunt A loose on the Brookside streets.

"Well, I'm not sure when I'll be home," she said with all honesty. "But when I know, I'll call you just as I promised. I really have to go, Aunt A. Perhaps Candy could come into the store and talk to Sherri."

"Well, that's another thing. She still doesn't have her car, you see. So I told her you would give her a ride over and back sometimes," her aunt continued as though the matter were a settled issue.

"I'm not sure I can—" Adding chauffeur to her day's schedule right now seemed an impossibility. Most days for the next three weeks she'd be at Reeves House and she didn't want her days restricted by being responsible for someone else's transportation. And with Sherri agreeing to be there to open the store for her, Ivy had hoped to go straight out to Reeves House without coming in at all a few mornings.

"It won't be forever, Ivy. Just until she can get

her car back from David. Remember, 'those who help the needy honor God,''' Aunt A concluded with a Proverb.

Ivy sighed, rummaging through her purse to make sure she had everything. Candy had been fired from more than one job; Ivy'd heard the tales from a teary Shirley. Now, of course, Ivy understood why Candy had lost the last one. Too many absences due to too many domestic problems didn't breed job stability.

''All right, Aunt A. But tell me—does Candy have any retail experience?''

Sherri breezed in and waved her good-morning. Ivy smiled hers while checking to see she'd left her good shears at the house or in her toolbox.

After putting her coat away, Sherri asked softly ''Do you want me to dismantle the sale table?''

Ivy nodded.

''Oh, Candy can learn anything, I'm sure,'' Aunt Arletta continued. ''And there's another thing. Shirley's apartment is getting awfully crowded. She has only the one bedroom, you remember.''

Ivy stopped her rummaging and clamped the phone closer to her mouth. ''Aunt Arletta, don't you dare. We don't have room for a long-term guest—''

''I wasn't going to do anything like that, Ivy,'' Arletta insisted, a bit too hastily for Ivy's peace of mind. ''But they have to find a place of their own and the boys have to get back into school, too. That's a real problem, Ivy, they need more clothes and things, so I was thinking…may Candy borrow your car? Just for today, Ivy. She really can't go back home to live, you know—she has to do it while her husband's gone to work and the sooner the better, don't you think?''

Ivy was hesitant over loaning her car again. But she could truly understand how helpless Candy would feel by being so dependent on others.

If a man has two cloaks... whispered her heart. Ivy paused. It wouldn't really put her out to loan Candy her car this week while she was driving the rental van. And if she could help get Candy on her feet, why not?

A customer stood about, giving Ivy a disgruntled stare at her lengthy time using the phone. She glanced at her watch. "All right, Aunt A. My extra key is in my bedroom desk center drawer. I'll think about the rest. Gotta go."

She hung up the phone and went to help the customer. She was never going to get going.

Finally on her way to Reeves House an hour later, Ivy hoped to accomplish a bit more work than yesterday. Or the day before. Even though her problem was a happy one, she still had one in Gerry.

He always coaxed her to stray from whatever task she was involved in, enticed her with offers of morning coffee breaks, lunch trays in his office, or a peek at his snapshots from Europe. When he was around, she never quite accomplished everything on her list.

But she found it all fun and Gerry's attention stimulating.

"Aren't you ashamed of yourself, keeping me from my work?" she teased him the second day she was there. "Or are you waiting for another invitation to join the fun of removing wallpaper?"

"No, thanks. My last lesson in wallpaper removal was quite enough fun for me. I'll find my amusement in other forms, if you please. But why should I be ashamed for asking for your fellowship?" He smiled and ran a hand through his swag of moonlight blond hair; the gesture struck her as one of practiced grace, meant to capture her admiring gaze. "I won't be robbing anyone else by asking you to do something besides work, will I? You are working on my time, after all."

"I suppose I am," she said and returned his smile, dismissing the unflattering thought of his conceit. What did it matter if Gerry was a bit too aware of his good looks? It had been her experience to find that quality in most males.

Today Ivy was scraping old paint from a window section taken out of the attic when Gerry wandered upstairs toward noon. He stepped carefully over the debris, examined the work under way in the various rooms, then settled his back against a wall in the room where she worked, to observe for a while.

"Take a break, Ivy, and come outside for a stroll."

"I'd love to, Gerry, but this great old window frame needs to be stripped and finished. The contractor thinks he can reuse it."

"Sounds good. But you can do it later."

"Really, Gerry," she protested. "Don't you feel guilty at all in taking me away when there's all this work to be done?"

"No, why should I? The work will get done. But this pretty morning will never come again." He tugged at her hand like a beguiling little boy, smiling with the same quality. "I want to enjoy the company of a pretty, intelligent woman in an otherwise boring day."

What could she say after those flattering comments? Or do but agree? And she did want to go.

She loved the beauty of the grounds even in the dead of winter.

"Okay," she said, returning his grin like a kid playing hooky from school. "Let me wash my hands first."

Gerry tucked her arm through his as they strolled down one path and then another past shaped evergreens, winter-quiet flower beds, and graceful bare-branched trees that she recalled in autumn splendor. They talked of nothing much.

She took deep breaths of crisp morning air free of dust or stale odors and knew herself to be blessed. Not everyone had such opportunities. But as they ambled back, it came to mind that though the Reeves siblings owned this grand old mansion, it was Noah and his crew who kept its grounds in such lovely condition. They would take constant care in all seasons; Reeves House must represent a big account for The Old Garden Gate. For the first time she wondered what other estates Noah might service.

She hadn't seen Noah since New Year's Day. Not even at church. She frowned, realizing that only unusual circumstances would keep him away. Hmm... she'd ask her aunt about him as soon as she had the chance.

Or she could simply call him herself. She owed him a check anyway, for the decorating job at the law offices. That would be excuse enough. But she usually didn't do her accounts until the end of the month—her early payment to Matt before Christmas aside—and she didn't want to invite any further advances or give Noah the idea...the thought...

Oh, mercy, she didn't want to encourage Noah to think more of such a call than was business. Or give him another opportunity for a kiss. Or let him think she wanted more than friendship, even though she found him terribly attractive in spite of herself. Sometimes.

Most of the time.

Uh-oh. Maybe it was just as well not to worry where he was or what he was doing or let herself fidget because he hadn't been around of late. She ought to feel happy he'd found something else to occupy his time for a while. Or somebody.

Yet that thought didn't make her feel all too easy, either.

"Ivy?" Gerald said, jerking her gaze around.

"Oh." Glancing at his half-narrowed eyes, she realized he'd spoken to her more than once. "Sorry, Gerry. What did you say?"

They paused at a small footbridge across a trickle of water. She gazed over the railing at the smooth stones beneath, thinking of the wearing away of all the rough edges it took to sand them down. How long did it take? Years?

"What were you thinking that you were so far away?" Gerry asked, moving them on.

"Oh, nothing too earth-shattering, I guess." She pulled a deep breath. "Just business concerns."

"Business concerns, is it? Well, that's a good reason to follow my suggestion."

"Oh? And what was that?"

"What I said was, why don't you move into Reeves House for the duration."

"I beg your pardon?" She blinked in surprise at his impulsiveness and stopped in the middle of the path. He certainly liked doing things on the spur of the moment. "Are you serious?"

"Sure, why not?" He leaned against a huge boulder, brushing the surface to invite her to share it. She allowed him to lift her up and she sat, dangling her jean-clad legs.

"Well, it's a bit unusual. You employ my services to decorate your house."

"Yes, I admit it is unusual, but you know I'm interested in you, Ivy. I hoped we could take the time to get to know each other better. Why can't we bypass a lot of the dating thing?"

"How do you mean?"

"Well, as to that—you'd be on the spot bright and early each morning without the morning commute. You'll begin the morning fresh. And we certainly have room for you. Then we can mix business with pleasure with no guilt tags."

"Ah, business and pleasure...what sort of mixing did you have in mind?"

He cast her an impatient glance. "Oh, all on the innocent side, Ivy, if that's what is worrying you. You are a bit of a throwback, aren't you, darling?"

"I suppose I am, compared to most of the women you must meet, but..."

"No, not that I don't find you terribly attractive—" he caressed her cheek with one finger "—but I simply meant we can enjoy our evenings free of outside hassles. We can do whatever takes our fancy, have dinner out or in, take in a movie or a jazz concert. We can get to know one another in closer quarters."

She glanced down at her folded hands, trying to control her excitement. He'd declared a romantic interest. He wanted to see her in a daily setting, to see if they were compatible. He'd asked her to fly to

Switzerland at Christmas, and now this. Would he ask her a third time if she continued to refuse him?

"But Gerry, I do have a business to run."

"It would only be for a week or so, Ivy. Can't your assistant, what's-her-name, take care of things for a couple of days? Or don't you trust her?

"Her name is Sherri, and yes, I trust her."

"And there's nothing to stop you from running into town when you need to. Think of it as reverse travel."

That was all true. Why couldn't she stay in this wonderful old house for a few days? It would give her a long overdue break. While running off to Switzerland had been out of the question over Christmas, a few days at Reeves House was doable.

"I would hate to overburden the Marshalls," she murmured a last objection.

He laughed at her absurdity. "They won't be. One guest in residence is much less than the dozen or two expected when we start using Reeves House as a small retreat and conference center." His smile was cajoling. "Come on, Ivy, say yes."

"Well, I can't promise, but I'll see what I can do."

Driving home late that afternoon, Ivy thought about the invitation. She'd thought about little else all afternoon. She really wanted to accept the offer.

In addition, Gerry seemed honestly excited about the prospect. And if she hoped to fit into his social circles completely, if she and Gerry were to become a couple, she would be faced with these sudden whims of his from time to time. She didn't mind that so much; this was the life-style for which she'd prayed.

But living at Reeves House for a few days did

present her with puzzles to solve. Leaving the store in Sherri's hands wasn't near the complication she thought leaving Aunt Arletta alone might become. Her aunt was growing older; who would be there at night if she had a sudden need for assistance? Who would run her to church and the grocery store?

Ivy couldn't ignore her own truth. If Ivy were to marry, their living arrangements would change, and that was a fact.

"Never mind," she muttered aloud. Wherever she went, Aunt A would go with her. But she couldn't think about that just now. She wasn't ready to deal with it. It was enough to think about the present exciting offer.

"Lord, you're the one who holds all the answers in the grand scheme of things..."

A chuckle bubbled up. For once, she'd just let the future take care of itself and dream of how life might be if she married Gerald Reeves.

It would be a far cry from life in an old ramshackle trailer.

Now, from what crack in her armor had that thought popped? However did Noah get into the picture?

"Well, I won't think about him, either," she muttered aloud once more. Rather, she'd think about who at church she could prevail upon to agree to be on call for Aunt Arletta while she was at Reeves House.

Kelly wasn't as free as she once was; she had Scott to consider these days.

Then she grinned, feeling as ornery as a kid out for revenge. Maybe she would ask Noah. The Old Garden Gate was still in its resting phase and he didn't have all that much to do. And Noah would more than likely jump at a chance to share the dinner table with Aunt Arletta if she offered to cook his favorite meal. An extra dose of Aunt Arletta's company would teach him not to encourage any more of her antics.

But then, she'd owe him a favor and that would never do. She couldn't take the chance that he'd misinterpret her request.

She sighed. Too bad—but no.

That left Candy, now staying only two doors away, who needed to borrow her car. It was the simplest solution and she'd only be gone a few days, after all. Surely Candy could bail Aunt A out of a jam if there was a need for it.

Ivy made several calls as soon as she arrived home that evening. Sherri and Emily had inventoried one whole section of the store. And yes, Candy had come in to see her.

"What do you think of her?"

"Oh..."

"Honestly, now."

"She's eager to work, I suppose, but she has so many problems. Ivy, is Candy one of your Aunt A's little lambs?"

Ivy swallowed her groan as Aunt Arletta bustled into her bedroom, murmuring, "Dinner in five minutes." If Sherri noticed how helpless Candy sometimes appeared, it no longer seemed like such a good idea to ask Candy to be on call for Aunt Arletta.

Ivy nodded to her aunt, then muttered into the phone. "Yeah, that's right. Just do what you can for her, please Sherri?"

That threw her back to square one.

Well, maybe she would think of some solution.

Maybe Aunt Arletta wouldn't mind being on her own for a few days, if Ivy explained it all in the best possible way.

Yes, she'd just have to help her aunt understand the importance of this special invitation. It could change her entire future.

Chapter Seventeen

After dinner, Ivy sorted through her clothes, trying to decide what to take with her if she should go, wondering if she could manage an hour's shopping the next day for something new.

The thing to do was simply tell Aunt A of Gerry's invitation. She'd think of someone herself. It wasn't as though she were going across the world. Only a few miles, really.

"I wish you'd call Noah, Ivy," her aunt said suddenly, out of the blue, poking her head around Ivy's bedroom door. "I'm worried about him."

"Noah?" The request caught her off guard. "Why, what's up with Noah?"

"He has a bad cold. That trailer of his is so old and drafty it was bound to happen. Only the good Lord knows how he's lived through two winters there without coming down with pneumonia before now. But when he called the church today to say he couldn't drive the bus for tomorrow's senior citizens' outing, I knew that meant he's really under the weather. I don't suppose we could—"

"If he feels that awful he won't want company, Aunt Arletta." Sitting on the side of her bed, she picked up her extension. "I'll, um, I'll just phone him."

The phone rang a long time. Ivy frowned, biting her lip. Aunt Arletta watched her expectantly. She shrugged, letting her aunt know she hadn't received an answer.

Finally the answering machine kicked on and she left a message to return a call when he felt better. She tried his truck phone next, without results.

"Maybe Matt?" Aunt Arletta's gaze filled with concern.

"All right," Ivy said, punching in the numbers. It was worth the extra call to make Aunt A happy.

"I haven't heard from Noah in a couple of days, Ivy," Matt said. "He's probably just out in the barn."

"Sure, that's probably it. Okay, thanks, Matt."

Hanging up the receiver, Ivy tapped it a moment, gazing at her aunt. Aunt Arletta stared at her with worried eyes.

"That's not like him, Ivy..."

Ivy bit her lip. There probably was no need to feel so concerned. Noah was one man who could take care of himself.

But the barn had a phone and so did the office trailer; his phone system kicked from one to another. If he was there, why didn't he answer? If he wasn't, did that mean he'd merely made an excuse not to drive the bus? But that was unlike him, too.

Just in case the line hadn't transferred, she tried the office number. Still nothing.

Only seconds from hanging up, she finally heard the receiver lift and a gruff mumble. She gave a relieved nod, and saw her aunt sigh.

"Noah?" It didn't sound like him. The velvety voice came through like a bear with a sore nose.

"Yeah?"

"I called a few moments ago but there was no answer. Aunt A's been worried about you."

"Just a cold. Didn't hear the phone."

That wasn't like Noah, either. He was usually very alert and quick to answer. "Noah, how long have you been sick?"

"Day or two. Don't worry, sweet Ivy vine, I'm wearing my coat."

"Your coat? Are you in the barn, then?"

"Nope. Catchin' up with office stuff."

Something didn't sound right. In his voice or his speech. Why would he need his coat inside his office? Unless…

"Don't you have the heat switched on? Noah?"

"Heat. It's broken."

"Well, if your office heater is broken, why are you out there?" She wondered if he was feverish. "It sounds to me as though you need to be in bed."

"Been in bed. Boring—" A harsh cough erupted, and Ivy heard him shift away from the phone. It lasted a full minute.

"Noah—"

"Lonesome out here, Ivy," he finally confessed barely above a whisper.

"Noah—" She stopped abruptly, making up her mind rapidly as another cough began. "Noah, are you listening? I want you to go back to your house trailer now." Then for emphasis, "Aunt Arletta says so. Get under the blankets. Stay warm. I'll be there in less than an hour, all right?"

She hung up the phone, not sure if he'd taken in her instructions or not.

"I'll go with you, Ivy dear."

"Um, not this time, Aunt Arletta. I think I'll run Noah to one of those all-night clinics to see a doctor. I don't know when I'll be home."

"Well, you might as well bring him back here afterward," Aunt Arletta called as she swung through the door.

Ivy sighed. There was no way she could take herself out to Reeves House for an extended stay.

Gerry would be ruffled for sure. Maybe even angry. But she couldn't let Noah shift for himself when he was sick. Never mind her own worried concern, Aunt Arletta wouldn't like it. She wouldn't rest well and then, neither would Ivy.

She'd explain it to Gerry and surely he'd understand.

Forty minutes later Noah gazed at her through bleary eyes as he stumbled back from letting her through the door. Sampson streaked off to hide behind a chair.

Oh, bother. She'd forgotten the cat.

She turned her attention to the two-legged problem. His heavy shirt gaped wide and hung outside his jeans; underneath, his sweat-stained thermal undergarment looked as though it had seen better days. His skin looked flushed above his unshaven jaw. She wondered how high his temperature ran.

Still, he tried to smile.

"If I'd known that telling you I was lonesome would get you out here I'd have said so every day, Ivy."

"Have you seen a doctor?"

"Didn't get around to it. It's only a little cold."

"Mmm... Well, get your coat, your pajamas and a change of clothes, Noah. I'm taking you home with me."

"Hmm...that sounds like an interesting invitation." His gaze took on a teasing light.

"Don't be silly." Sampson began twisting around her ankles, mewing his hunger. "I'm just not leaving you out here in this cold to fend for yourself, that's all."

"You love me that much, huh?"

"Don't get any ideas, Noah. You're sick."

"Not that sick, Ivy vine. Admit it. You care about me."

"Yeah, about as much as lukewarm milk. But if I hadn't come out to see about you, Aunt Arletta would've kept me up all night or sent out the search dogs."

He started to chuckle, but went into a coughing spasm instead. It hurt her to listen. Stepping forward, she placed her palm against his back. His body heat burned her skin through the layers of his clothing.

"Not that I mind, Ivy," he said, straightening. "I think it's kinda nice you came all the way out here to see me at this time of night. But why are you playing mother hen all of a sudden?"

"It's for Aunt Arletta's sake," Ivy insisted. She wasn't about to admit to owning a single mother-hen feather. Not she. "She's worried about you. Now come on—oh, never mind."

She marched down the narrow hall past stacked dishes in the sink and into his rumpled bedroom. Searching through his chest, she found clean underclothes. Then she opened another drawer and grabbed heavy socks and a flannel shirt.

''Noah, I can't find any clean jeans.''

''Out here,'' he mumbled in a croak. ''Didn't get 'em put away from the laundry.''

''Well, let's have them,'' she said as she returned to the living room. She searched through cupboards to find a couple of cans of cat food. ''I suppose we'll have to take Sampson with us for now. Noah, why don't you get your toothbrush while I get a bag for these?''

''Okay. And as long as you're gathering stuff, Ivy, would you mind running next door to the office and picking up those folders on my desk? Trying to catch up on my computer entries when you called. Gotta pay bills.''

Another coughing spell stopped her from telling him to forget it. It was going to be another long night. She seemed destined to spend the last hours of a day in Noah's company lately. And sure enough, at close to midnight, Ivy put Noah to bed—in her room.

''Really sweet of you to give up your bed, Ivy vine,'' he mumbled with exhaustion.

They'd spent nearly two hours in the clinic where he was diagnosed with an upper respiratory infection, then another hour in an all-night drugstore to fill his prescriptions.

''Sweet? Not hardly. I'm just not about to let all this effort go to waste. Besides, I'd have to answer to Aunt Arletta if I'd let you get pneumonia.'' Never mind that when the doctor had told Ivy Noah didn't have pneumonia, she'd sent up a silent prayer of thanks. A deep tenderness welled up inside her at the sight of his droopy eyes; the medication was working. His usually busy hands lay slack outside the blanket, and she had to smother the urge to pick one up and hold it until he drifted off.

She cleared her throat. "If you don't get well soon Aunt A will have my hide. And Chad, not to mention Haley and Scott will fuss up a storm when they find out you're out of commission for a while. I hear they've sent out another basketball challenge."

"Yep. Next week," he said, his husky mumble almost a whisper. "You comin' to cheer for me?"

"We'll talk about that later," she soothed softly, hovering, wanting to brush a lock of his dark hair off his brow. Knowing she should leave, but unable to make herself move. "Now go to sleep."

Later as she let herself slowly relax into sleep on the couch, she tried to mentally number all the things she had on her to-do list, including letting Gerry know she couldn't possibly move out to Reeves House, no matter how sensible it sounded, no matter how much she wanted to accept. But her last conscious thought was, *Please, Lord. Touch Noah's aching body and drive the infection from it. Please bless him with healing....*

A few days later, Ivy drove out to Reeves House without even checking in with Sherri first. She'd catch her very able assistant later. The morning drive had become a pleasant routine, every curve and bump in the road familiar after she left route sixty-nine.

Accepting Noah's presence in her small apartment

had become routine, too; but she was getting mighty tired of sleeping on the front room couch and tiptoeing around her own bedroom to gather clean clothes and cosmetics. But she had to chuckle—sharing living quarters for more than a few hours with a male made unusual demands on both her and Aunt Arletta. And what else could she have done?

Of course, Aunt Arletta loved it. She had someone to mother and fuss over all day long, and company, too. Ivy hadn't had a single phone call from her since Noah moved in, when she often had five or six. And no phone calls from anyone else, for that matter. At least it made for a smoother workday at Reeves House.

But Gerry hadn't been pleased. He'd flown to Chicago the day before yesterday, barely telling her he'd be out of town for a couple of days. She only hoped she could make him understand—Aunt Arletta's natural compassion wasn't to be halted or blocked. And why should it? Wasn't that very caring what the scriptures directed for believers?

There was no way Ivy could've left Noah to fend for himself when he needed help, and she hadn't wanted to, anyway. Ivy had been the recipient of Aunt A's loving care too many times.

Yet Ivy refused to think about the excitement that built as she drove home each night. The knowledge that she had two people waiting for her when she got there, one a good-looking, quick-witted man who kept her laughing with his quips.

She'd missed having brothers, she told herself. Having Noah in residence served to show how it might have been growing up with siblings, she decided. That was the logical answer to her wanting to rush home these past several nights—the mere novelty. It had nothing to do with warm brown eyes.

It was only...she didn't want to grow too used to having him there. Or her aunt, too happily content with the present arrangement.

Later in the morning, Ivy flipped through the new fabric swatches with Barbara, pulling out the possibilities as they sat on the second-story lounge floor. Ivy insisted she was too dusty to occupy a chair. Above them, the noise of the new windows being installed raged.

"That's nice, there," Barbara murmured, spying a turquoise blue that almost matched the color of her eyes. "Soft. Don't think I'd tire of that very soon. It might be a good choice for one of the Dwelling bedrooms if I don't choose it for myself. What do you think, Ivy?"

"It's beautiful and I love it, but it's rather expensive for the Dwelling, don't you think? Even at my cost I think the budget committee might scream over that kind of expenditure when more practical matters need to be attended to first. Besides, it'll be months before we have to choose bedroom furnishings for the Dwelling. I don't think the house search has turned up with anything solid, yet. Too bad, too."

"Why is that?" Barbara asked.

"Oh, it's just that I know someone who's in the position of needing a little boost right now, although she's not in the older generation as we've pictured the Dwelling to serve. And she's not in a really desperate situation. She has some place to live, at least."

"Oh, my." Barbara's eyes grew round. "You actually know someone like that personally? I've never really met anyone...I mean...um, I've just read about these situations. I'm sorry, Ivy. That made me sound like such a snob."

"It's all right Barbara. Not everyone can be born into poverty," she joked.

Barbara laughed before sobering. "Well, the things I've been reading! Not all abused wives are poor, either. I was shocked after I found out the troubles of another friend of ours. She was so ashamed to admit to being a battered woman and none of us ever dreamed of her situation. That's when Toni and I had the idea to start Deborah's Dwelling. It seems the up-and-out are as needy as the down-and-out for a safe place to, um, withdraw until..."

"Yes, the committee has discussed the Dwelling's purpose more than once," Ivy commented. Odd. She'd thought the plan for the Dwelling had come from Gerry, and said so.

"Oh, no. But Gerry's always into charity works. He likes sitting on the boards and all the doors it opens. He was looking around for something new to get into when Toni and I broached our idea."

Ivy nodded, and continued to discuss the merits of one fabric swatch over another. It made her think. Gerry worked at gaining the funding for a new charity, Barbara galvanized her friends into supporting it, Noah and Aunt Arletta selflessly gave up much of their time to help others, and she hadn't really been willing to loan a friend her car.

"If a man has two cloaks..." drifted through her thoughts. Then it hit her. She'd been willing to help Candy when it cost her nothing personally or only as a sop for Aunt Arletta's need to help. But her own heart hadn't been involved in real compassion.

Oh, Lord, forgive my selfishness and self-absorbed

state of mind. Open my eyes.... She'd tell Aunt A to offer Candy her car as long as she needed it, just as soon as she got home.

"Actually," Barbara again spoke while holding up another swatch to the light, "the search committee has found a house that most of us like. It's close to the old Westport area."

"Oh? Is it one they've talked about? What's it like?"

"Well, yes, it has been discussed. The problem is, it's rather small for the purposes. But now the committee thinks they could buy the property next to it and the adjoining vacant lot on the corner."

"That's interesting. Rather like a compound."

"But if we bought both houses and the lot we couldn't pay for them all outright. We'd have to ask for loans...."

"Is that all?" Ivy said with a chuckle. "Dealing with a mortgage loan shouldn't be a problem, Barbara. But surely the projections can tell us where we stand on funds."

"I suppose. Speaking of the fund drives—"

"Here you two are," Gerry said, coming up the stairs two at a time. "I've been looking for you, Ivy—I want you to look at some paintings."

"Oh, hi, Gere," Barbara greeted her brother. "Back from the big town already? I was just telling Ivy the latest from the property search committee."

"Yes," he paused, looking at Ivy directly while ignoring his sister. "Wasn't much point in hanging around there when I have more interesting things going on at home. The Sanderses send their regards."

"That's nice, Gerry," Ivy replied. "Did they agree to help sponsor the Dwelling?"

"Yes, they did. Come downstairs and I'll tell you all about it."

"Thanks, Gerry, but I really have to get going," she said. She gathered up the swatches that Barbara had discarded, and stood. "I have to put in an appearance at the store today. Don't want to lose Sherri by neglect, you know."

"I'll excuse you only if you promise me to come out to dinner tonight," Gerry insisted. "I'll pick you up promptly at seven."

"All right," she said, and smiled. Evidently she had regained his good opinion.

Chapter Eighteen

Ivy breezed through the apartment door well before five. Triumphantly, she carried with her an expensive new dinner dress. Her pearl stud earrings and the pearl ring she'd received at Christmas would be just the things to wear with it. She hoped it would please Gerry; she hoped he'd notice she wore his gift.

"Is that you, Ivy?" her aunt called from the kitchen. "My, you're home early for a change. Did you close the store already?'

"Yes, Aunt Arletta, it's me," she said, rounding the kitchen door. "And I left Sherri and Emily to close up."

"Hiya, sweet Ivy vine," Noah croaked with a grin. But in truth he sounded much better. He must be feeling better, too, she noted, because he had his files spread out before him like a fan and his checkbook close at hand. A notebook computer, plugged in and running sat just beyond.

"Hiya, back, froggy," she teased, denying the leap her heart took at sight of him. "Sitting up and working? My, my, we'll have you ready to shoot baskets again in no time. Are you sure you want to postpone your game with Scott 'til next week?"

"Sure 'nuff, honey. Gotta get my breath back." His gaze softened as he looked at her, giving her the impression the subject of his declaration wasn't the basketball game. Pleasurable warmth flooded through her all the way to her toes.

The phone rang and Aunt Arletta picked it up. "The Old Garden Gate," she chirped into the line.

In the act of leaving the kitchen, Ivy stopped and reversed her direction. She glanced from the small computer to her aunt and back to the computer again.

Wait a minute. That slim notebook looked just like hers. She didn't use it much because she much preferred to use the larger equipment at the store; this one usually lay stored under her bed. And there were far more files in front of him than she remembered gathering from his trailer.

"What—?"

"Hope you don't mind, Ivy. Had my calls forwarded here," Noah said on a sheepish note. "Candy ran out to the tree farm for me and picked up some more things."

"Candy did?" With her car, no doubt.

"Yes. Oh, by the way, Candy's going to work for me. She has a hankering to get into the plant business."

"Oh, that's just dandy. After I went to all that trouble to make a place for her at Wall's Intrigue. Why, Sherri expected her to start work this week. What happened?"

"Aw, I am sorry, Ivy. Look, I didn't know you

were counting on her, but she took my offer so I had her start by running a few errands for me.''

''Uh-huh. Well, just remind her I want my car back by the end of the week.''

''Aunt Arletta let me borrow your notebook, too. Just for a day or two 'til I go home. Aunt A is doing double duty as receptionist.''

''And having a fine time doing it, too, I see.'' Ivy was torn between real irritation at having her home turned into Noah's office and his borrowing everything in sight including Aunt Arletta, and outright laughter. Why was it he had to be so earth-shatteringly charming while doing it? ''Nobody could ever accuse you of letting any grass grow under your feet,'' she intentionally punned.

''Ouch,'' he groaned.

''It's for you, Mr. Thornton,'' Aunt Arletta said formally, handing over the phone with an affirmative nod. ''It's Mr. Pierce.''

Noah gave Ivy a wink and took the receiver. ''Hi, John. Yeah, I have your landscape plans all ready for you to look at anytime....'' Noah concentrated on his business call and turned to look at the kitchen wall calendar. ''You're first up in the spring.''

As Ivy began to leave again she brushed against the table. A file went flying, spilling its contents all over the floor.

''Really, Ivy,'' her aunt protested at her clumsiness. Noah looked up just as she bent to gather it all up.

Several papers slid under the table. Ivy went to her knees to retrieve them. Business bills, mostly. Receipts. Black-and-white print, colored logos and symbols. A green clover leaf, an acorn, a gold heart. A receipt for $359 paid to a charity for children with terminal diseases, dated September tenth. Forty-five dollars paid to the same, dated in November. A clutch of papers, all the same kind, stapled together, the one on top showing the same foundation's imprint. A mortgage payment schedule.

She reached for a last paper. A receipt, printed with a familiar jewelry store logo. The store from which her ring had come.

"Just a moment, John." Trying to maintain his conversation, Noah suddenly shoved his way under the table, grabbing the papers from her hand. "Thanks, Ivy."

Letting them go as quickly as he grasped, she rose in startled suddenness. Had Noah given her the ring? Her head banged against the table edge.

"Oohh..." She sat on the floor with a thump.

Noah gave her a swift glance, said, "John, everything's fine. I'll call you tomorrow," and hung up the phone. He knelt beside her. "Sorry, Ivy, honey. Didn't mean to—"

"Are you hurt, Ivy?" Aunt Arletta asked as she hovered nearby.

"I'm all right," she mumbled, blinking against her smarting eyes. "Just seeing stars."

She sat a moment to allow her spinning head to calm down. Aunt Arletta handed her a damp cloth. What had gotten into Noah? So she'd noticed a couple of bills, and evidence of his generosity toward a favored charity. What in that would upset him? Every business had bills. But she no longer questioned why he lived in such modest means, and those bills proved her long held suspicions—the man wasn't too swift as a businessman.

"So I make you see stars? You can return the favor anytime, Ivy." Noah took the damp cloth from her hand and gently patted her forehead. His eyes shone with soft amusement. "You want to?"

"No," she insisted, deciding to retreat with dignity. She wasn't ready to ask him if he'd given her the ring she'd grown to love. She could tackle that subject later. Pushing his hand away and rising to stand, she announced, "I'm going to retire to my own room now."

His laughter followed her down the hall. By all that was precious, she'd send him home tomorrow. He'd recovered quite enough to take care of himself.

The evening had turned colder as Gerry brought her home. He walked her to her door, his hand at her elbow. From the front window, a lamp glow shone through the drape.

He tipped his head and leaned toward her, a kiss his obvious intent. Ivy lifted her chin, obligingly.

Just short of his goal, he hesitated. From the corner of her eye, Ivy caught swift movement. The window drape twitched.

Gerry's momentum abruptly halted as her door swung wide.

"Uh, sorry, Ivy," Noah said. But his gaze wasn't sorry. "Evening, Gerry. Nice night, huh? Um, just wanted to, um, get something out of your car, Ivy. Be back in a sec."

Gerry stiffened, his body imitating a block of ice.

Noah pushed past them unhurriedly, heading for the parking lot. He hadn't offered an apology to Gerry, she noticed. And the winter night wasn't nice at all; it was damp and cold. Fuming, Ivy watched him disappear around the corner of a building.

"Gerry..." What could she say?

"I'll say good-night, Ivy." She wondered how he could talk through his clenched teeth at all. "Tomorrow?"

"It's Saturday, but I'll be there. Early."

Ivy strode into her apartment and swirled to face the open door. She stood firm against the cold blustery wind with a strength of fire to match. The minute Noah came through it, looking as innocent as a smug bean counter hiding half the beans, she let him have it.

"You presumptuous rag! You did that on purpose."

"What?" he began, closing the door. "What did I do?"

"You know very well what you did. This time, the last time, and the time before that."

"Well, at least I'm consistent. Do I get points for that?"

"Oh, yeah. You get points all right. I'll give you points right off the top of your head if you ever do it again."

"Okay, Ivy vine, don't get in a twit. But that's an interesting thought on giving me points. Tell me what I did."

"You interrupted my date intentionally, as if you didn't know. Just like an eight-year-old. Gerry thinks you do nothing but hang around my apartment. He thinks you—"

Ivy narrowed her eyes, not willing to put into words the loving affection she saw in Noah's brown eyes. The fact that his gaze held a teasing quality as well only added fuel to her fire, but he knew how to keep his own firmly in place. Her ire didn't seem to faze him.

"You—" How could she say that Gerry thought Noah was in love with her? She had no intention of opening that can of worms.

"Yeesss?"

Pursing her lips, she tried one last time. "Gerry will never understand that you...even though I try to explain—"

Not a jot of remorse shone from those brown eyes. "Oh, bother. Just never mind! Just leave me alone, d'you hear?"

Spinning on her high-heeled pump, she marched down the hall to her bedroom. Clothes he'd discarded lay across her lone chair, his brush lay on her dresser top, next to hers. The smoothly made bed hadn't been ruffled yet tonight; it looked as though fresh linens had been put on. Courtesy of Aunt Arletta, she was sure.

Oh, yes. Aunt Arletta loved spoiling Noah Thornton. But Ivy'd had just about enough. Swiftly, she gathered up his jeans and shirt, his pj bottoms and brush, and rolled them together. Once more to a silent marching beat, she stormed out to the living room and shoved them into Noah's hands.

"And you get the couch. Tomorrow you go home, mister. Got that? Now stay out of my life!"

"Ivy, why won't you give me Matt's number?" Barbara begged while watching Ivy paste wallpaper samples on one of the bedroom walls.

"Because I gave my word to Matt that I wouldn't, Barbara, as I told you," Ivy said over her shoulder. "I can't betray the trust of one of my artists. But you know how chatty Aunt Arletta is, and Aunt A loves nothing better than to—''

''Thanks, Ivy, you're a peach.'' Barbara, her blue eyes sparkling, made a dash from the room. ''Catch you later.''

Ivy chuckled. Later in the afternoon, she wandered downstairs for a cup of tea. Mrs. Marshall waved her into Gerry's office-study, telling her Gerald would take tea with her.

She knocked and stepped through. ''Gerry?''

He wasn't there. But his computer was on, the screen saver blinking with flying kites. His phone rang, and after a moment the answering machine picked it up. ''Hi, Gerry, Ron here.''

Ivy didn't recognize the voice. ''Just wanted to let you know your bid on the second Westport house was accepted at the price you offered.'' He quoted numbers. ''The sellers were disappointed in the low offer, but they accepted it with the stipulation the house was for the Dwelling. Now we get closure on all three properties and we're in business.''

The machine clicked off. Excited, Ivy turned as Gerry came into the room. ''Did you hear that, Gerry? The Dwelling compound is taking shape. That was our real estate broker with news of the acceptance of our bid on the second house.''

''Really?'' A momentary wariness came into his gaze. ''Ron or Wayne? When did he call?''

''Um, Ron, I think. Just now. It's on your machine.''

Jubilant, Gerry sat down and eagerly leaned forward as he made phone connections. ''Hey, buddy.'' He picked up a pen and began to doodle. ''I hear we have the property. Yeah? Uh-huh. Uh-huh. All right, we're on. Next week. No need to delay. In fact, the quicker the better. Later, Ron."

"Who's Ron?" she asked, pouring tea into delicate china cups. She set one before him on top of his doodles. "I thought we were dealing with Wayne from Basics Realty."

"Well, we are," he said in his smooth tones. "The Dwelling foundation is dealing with Wayne. Ron is simply another real estate agent who does favors for me now and again. Sometimes he finds property that interests me."

"Wow, it sure happened a lot faster than I thought it would. The committee will be ecstatic to hear the properties are secured."

"Well, yeah. Essentially, that's it. But don't say anything to anyone yet, all right? Let's keep it quiet until we have it all wrapped up."

"Ivy." Barbara popped her head through the door. "There's a guy here who's delivering a couple of packages. Said he needs your signature."

"Coming."

A few minutes later, Ivy went through to the kitchen, intent on heating up her tea. The Marshalls sat at the table, signing papers. Gerry stood watching behind Mrs. Marshall as she finished her signature.

"And one more, please, my dear Grace. Tom, you're finished except for your signature on this check."

"Good," Tom answered. "When do we get our money, Mr. Gerry? How long 'til this property turns over? Last time it took too long, if you ask me. Can't retire to the Virgin Islands without money, y'know."

"Your retirement nest egg is building fast enough, you greedy beggar. Just do your job, keep your mouth shut, and you'll get your share when Deborah's Dwelling buys it. But it'll take a few weeks."

What did he mean, when Deborah's Dwelling bought it? What property were they speaking of, the Westport houses or something new? They hadn't talked of anything more than the initial purchase.

Gerry spotted her and calmly scooped up the papers. Confused, Ivy made no comment; she simply walked to the microwave oven and heated her tea. When she turned, Gerry had left the room and the Marshalls had gone about their own business.

She tried to concentrate on finishing her task upstairs, but the scene she'd witnessed smacked of something off-kilter. Gerry behaved almost guiltily. What was the matter?

It wasn't any of her business. This wasn't her home, she reminded herself. She should keep her thoughts to herself.

But Deborah's Dwelling was her business; she'd committed herself to the cause wholeheartedly and her reputation stood on the line with it. If something was to go wrong she should be aware of it and try to help right it.

The house quieted toward dusk. After packing up her tools for the day, she stood a long moment before knocking on Gerry's office door.

"Yes?"

"It's me, Gerry. I want to talk to you."

"All right, Ivy, but make it fast if you don't mind. I'm on my way out soon."

Ivy blinked at the coolness in his tone. What had happened to his desire to deepen their friendship into courtship?

"Well, I wanted to know more about the sale."

She moved into the center of the room. A room she knew well, now, but she recalled how impressed she'd felt the first time she'd seen it several months before. She cleared her throat. "Those properties. How long have you known about them?"

"Oh, for a while. Ron keeps a lookout for me on retainer."

"Toni said she'd found them, but it sounds as if you had more to do with it than the search committee."

"Some." He glanced up from behind the desk where he was putting things away, then locking the drawers.

"Then it was you who introduced the properties to the search committee?"

"Yeah, sure. What's wrong with that?"

Pausing a moment, she licked her dry lips. The questions looming higher were so hard to ask, but the horrible, niggling suspicions weren't to be denied.

"Gerry, the prices the committee quoted were much higher than what I heard Ron state. Which figure is correct? Who owns those properties?"

"Well, it's rather complicated, Ivy." He avoided looking at her.

"I'm listening. What's going on?"

"Just business. You wouldn't understand it."

"I understand most business transactions fairly well," she replied with quiet strength. "Try me."

"Come on, Ivy darling." Leaving a final folder atop his desk, he moved out from behind it and slid an arm across her shoulder. "Don't look so worried over it. Everything's moving along just fine and the Dwelling will get the properties no later than spring.

Then you ladies will have a blast with the remodeling and decorating. Think of all the accolades you'll receive for Wall's Intrigue when it's all done. Now you run along and gather up your things and we can leave together. I'll see you tomorrow evening, won't I?"

She let it go for the moment. Perhaps she was imagining things. "I suppose so."

A few minutes later she came to the bottom of the stair, her heavy tool bag and purse slung over one shoulder, and looked around for Gerry. He was nowhere in sight and the lower floor lay in shadowed silence. She'd just take a moment to call Aunt Arletta, she decided, to tell her she was on the way home.

Entering the office, she let her bags slide to the floor just inside the door and then went around the desk, snapping on the light as she picked up the phone. Aunt Arletta's cheery voice answered, as Ivy's attention focused on the yellow pad with the doodles Gerry had made earlier. Dollar signs and numbers she recognized as the quotes from Ron. Subtractions and heavily imprinted circles around the bottom line. A hefty difference.

The top number was the one Toni had quoted the Dwelling needed for the complete trio of properties.

"Just me, Aunt A. I'm leaving now. Uh-huh, in the next five minutes."

Gerry pushed the door half-open to ask, "Ready, Ivy? I'll see you out."

"Almost, Gerry," she put her hand over the receiver. He nodded, and disappeared beyond the door. Her gaze returned to the doodled equation.

The folder in front of her held a Deborah's Dwelling label. Without a second's conscious thought of prying, she flipped it open. Printed forms lay on top, with a style and format she'd not seen. An income statement from Deborah's Dwelling Foundation made out to Gerald Reeves. The amount was staggering.

"Aunt A, I have to go," she muttered before hanging up the phone. She picked up the statement to read it again.

"Ivy, I suggest you put that away now," Gerald said calmly, but with force. She hadn't heard him reenter the room.

"What is this, Gerry?" She felt the shock drain the blood from her face. "Why are you drawing money from the Dwelling funds?"

"I draw a salary," he stated matter-of-factly. "As director."

"But no one else on the committee earns a penny! They volunteer their time."

"Yes they do, and the foundation is very grateful. But I, as chairman of the board and director, earn a fee."

"This?" She waved the paper statement aloft. "This is what the foundation pays you? What's it for, a one-time-only fee or an annual one? It's rather exorbitant, don't you think?"

"Exorbitant? Not at all, not for all I do. Surely you know what directors of large companies earn."

"But this is a nonprofit organization! A charity."

"So?"

"Does everyone know you take a salary of this size? And you take it from the top, I suppose?"

"I said you wouldn't understand. It's business, Ivy. Of course I take my salary up front. I can hardly work without personal capital."

"Well, how much of the donations trickles down, huh? Only last week, the property committee was crying the blues over scraping together every last dollar they could to merely take the first step. Toni said we were short by thousands and it might take some time yet to get the three properties."

"That's pretty much true. But after the funds come in from the Valentine's Day event, we should be able to cover it."

"At what price, Gerry? At the price Ron quoted?"

For the first time, he began to look uncomfortable. "Well, not exactly, Ivy. The property actually has been bought already. But I'm sure Deborah's Dwelling will get them in the end. By spring, I absolutely promise."

She stared at him as cold realization brought all the pieces of the puzzle together. "The Marshalls bought the three properties, didn't they? For a low-ball price with this Ron's help? What do you expect the foundation to pay for them, hmm, Gerry? How much do you get out of the deal? There are laws—"

"Everything I do is perfectly legal, my dear Ivy."

"Legal? I'm not sure about that. But I'm sure it's not moral, Gerry. How could you—?"

"Don't come on to me with your holier-than-thou attitude," he said, his words near a shout. Two bright spots of anger colored his cheeks. "Lots of people do it. You're in business, you know there are ways and means to play the numbers. You should try it sometime and make a real profit. That's the only way one can make any money these days."

"I won't make it dishonestly."

"I told you, I do what I do legally. Do you think I'd be fool enough to leave my back uncovered?"

"But Gerry..." Her heart hurt with what she was hearing. "What good is it to gain a whole world of profits if you lose your soul in the process?"

"You and your high-minded Noah! I swear the two of you are in league with each other."

"Why do you bring Noah into this?"

Gerry laughed in a nasty way. "Noah? Why not Noah? He's in the thick of it, let me tell you. You think he is perfectly innocent in some of the business deals we've made together in the past? Well, you just open your eyes, Ivy. He's played the game. How do you think he got his precious tree farm, anyway?"

Chapter Nineteen

Ivy drove home in a half-stunned state of mind. She'd left Reeves House with little recall of walking out the door. Mumbling something of a goodbye to Gerry without bothering to hide her deep disappointment in him, she'd simply picked up her things and left. How could she have been so blind? After all she'd faced with her past experiences, how could she have been so unaware of the signals?

She felt foolish and stupid. She'd let Gerry's wealth, smooth sophistication and big estate dazzle her, distract her from the truth.

She hadn't asked for God's wisdom!

Yet the discovery of Gerry's duplicity didn't give her even a tenth of the shattering sense of loss that hearing of Noah's involvement in the same sort of deception did. It gripped her stomach into an aching knot. Was it true?

Oh, Lord God, please let this be an awful dream. Not Noah…

Tears began then. Blinding, scalding tears. They

rolled down her cheeks to drip off her chin. Her throat clogging with them, she pumped the brake to pull off the road near a convenience store.

Coming to a complete stop, she laid her arm over the wheel and buried her face against it to let the sobs break.

Oh, Lord…what should I do? Help me! Help Aunt Arletta! Lord, you know Noah is the man of her choice for me. He's the only man in my life that she's ever really liked and she picked him. Her heart will break into a thousand pieces if Noah turns out to be a jerk like the others.

Who was she kidding? *Lord…I'm the one whose heart has shattered….*

She felt miserable enough to cover herself in sack-cloth and ashes. To remain single for the rest of her life and never contemplate marriage again.

Why is that so, Ivy? came the quiet, calm voice she equated with her heavenly director. *What about this ugly situation makes you so unhappy?*

This accusation of Gerry's—it would cause her to reexamine Noah's every kind act, every lovable trait that made her laugh, every sweet moment they'd shared.

Even the two passionate kisses? Had they been calculated and merely raw physical attraction? Had she misinterpreted the tenderness and love behind them?

She'd fallen in love with Noah, but until this very moment she'd denied it. Oh, yes, she had indeed, but she would no longer. How could she, when loving him hurt so much? How would she ever live through another heartbreak without losing all ability for trust again?

How, Lord? There will be nothing left of me....

In stark reality, she also knew this pain was oceans-deep worse than any other disappointment in her life. Not Eric, nor Dan, nor Leon had wounded her to this degree.

"Lord," she spoke aloud "I love Noah more than life. For once Aunt Arletta was right. Noah has filled my heart so full—he lifts my spirit. I'll be devastated if he's been dishonest, if he has used people so despitefully. Was I totally mistaken in him? What is true and what is false? I don't know anymore...."

Shivering with cold, she tried to calm herself. The only way to find out the truth was by confronting him. Could she know even then?

Above the clamoring confusion, past her waning sobs came the soft, clear voice. *Ivy...Ivy...listen to your heart...look for where you find Me and you will see the truth...search for the real treasures....*

Mopping her wet eyes, Ivy turned on her motor and headed toward town again. Deciding she'd better let her aunt know she was on her way home, she grabbed the car phone.

"Oh, Ivy dear, I'm so glad you called again," Aunt Arletta gushed before Ivy could explain anything. "There's a praise concert at church tonight with those visiting musicians, did you forget? But don't worry if you can't get home on time. Noah will take me."

Noah... All at once, her urge to see him overshadowed everything else. She had to hear the truth from his own lips.

"Aunt Arletta, I need to talk to Noah. It's very important. You tell him to stay put 'til I get there."

Ivy hung up before her aunt could argue. But

would Noah want to talk to her after the way she'd treated him? He'd been deeply wounded the other night when she'd told him to stay out of her life. That was a truth she couldn't deny. Perhaps what he felt for her was real after all.

Still, she had to hear what he had to say.

Noah waited for her outside on the grassy strip by the parking lot. Ivy saw him leaning against a tree, his breath vaporing in the cold air. Slowly getting out of the car, she scolded him, the sharp words popping out of her mouth without prior intention.

"You're just getting over an infection, Noah. You shouldn't be out here in this damp cold."

At her tone, a wariness flitted across his face. She bit her lip, instantly regretting her words. His wide mouth looked vulnerable without its usual humorous slant.

"Aunt A said you needed to discuss something with me?"

"Well, you needn't have waited outside." She tried softening her tone. "Let's go in."

"Let's not, Ivy. Whatever you want to talk about, let's get it over with here. You've got about ten minutes. Then I'll be heading to church."

Noah had a tough side to his character, she realized. He wasn't a pushover for anyone. Now his stance told her his defenses were up, and that it was her fault. Her harsh words of the other night remained between them.

Taking a deep breath, she heartily wished she had the gentle, sweetly teasing Noah back. "Um..."

"Spit it out, Ivy. What has your back up?"

"All right," she said, stiffening her resolve to face whatever came. "Out at Reeves House today, I, ah, heard something rather incriminating...and certainly unflattering to you... Oh, dash it, Noah. I want to know if it's true."

"What did you hear?" His usual deep velvet tones took on a rough quality.

"Gerry told me that you and he... Well, you see I questioned some of the business tactics of Deborah's Dwelling only to find out not everything is as it seems. All this money we've been working so hard to raise—all of it isn't going directly into the Dwelling's coffers. A great deal of it is going into private pockets. Gerry's, to be honest. Gerry said it was legal, that nonprofit corporations of this sort do it all the time—that you..."

"Yes?"

"He said such a business operation, you know—running charities and such for a high director's fee—was what gave you your landscaping business. He said you and he had been partners in this sort of thing."

She fell silent and he didn't respond. They stared at each other, the streetlight throwing part of his face into shadows. Her heart raced as though she'd sprinted a five-mile race.

When he continued to say nothing, she asked "Is it true?"

"Not in the sense you mean it, but I guess in the strictest of terms there's truth in the story. I made some money. But not every charity or nonprofit organization plays those games."

His words gave her such a sinking feeling she thought she might not be able to stand. *How could Noah be like Gerald?*

"But Gerry does? I...please explain, Noah," she

begged, her voice tight over her closed throat. "You must have some explanation about your own part in it."

"I do, but explanations take time. And they're useless unless you trust me, Ivy. How will you know whether I'm lying or telling the truth?"

She couldn't answer. Glib answers and covering over—she'd heard hundreds of excuses for inexcusable behavior before from the men to whom she'd been engaged.

How would she know if Noah was telling her the truth? Or would he merely tell *his* truth?

"You have no faith in me at all, do you Ivy?"

"I want to, but—"

"It's all right, Ivy vine." His voice sounded tired and worn as he pushed away from the tree. "I won't expect something from you that you can't give. Not your fault. I just wanted you so badly—I'd hoped we'd have a lifetime together, you and me and Aunt Arletta and the kids we might have. Guess I was wrong. Just plain too hardheaded to see it."

"What are you two kids doing out here in the cold?" Aunt Arletta asked, coming down the apartment sidewalk with Shirley. "Are you coming with us, Ivy?"

"No," Ivy struggled to answer. "I don't think I can, Aunt Arletta." How could she praise the Lord if she did nothing but cry throughout the service? She wanted nothing more than to run away and hide her pain and disillusionment. What was she to think?

Noah stepped away from the tree, and for a scant moment, the glow from the parking lot light shone on his face. The deep sorrow she saw in his brown eyes reflected her own misery. Without another word, he escorted the two elder ladies toward his truck.

"Well, I'll see you later," her aunt called over her shoulder.

"Sure, Aunt A. Later."

She didn't get past her own front door before a thought struck her. Gerry had deliberately maligned Noah's reputation to sidetrack his own guilt while Noah had avoided any mention of Gerry's wrongdoing. In the months she'd known him, Noah had never shown a single deceitful trait.

Pausing, she knew it wasn't over until she knew everything in specific detail; somehow, some way, she had to find out what had happened. Without entering the apartment, she headed back toward her car. Fifteen minutes later, she knocked on Matt's door.

"Ivy!" he said, opening wide. "I wasn't expecting you. Is there something wrong?"

"I don't know, Matt. I came because I need to hear the truth from someone and I hoped you'd know it."

"Come in and sit down," he said, limping over to his chair.

"Oh, Ivy, hello," Barbara said from her perch on the couch.

"Barbara?"

"Uh-huh." Barbara blushed slightly, and shot her a look of whimsical apology. "I came to see how my little buddy Chad's been."

Ivy pondered what to do while Matt directed Chad to play in his room. After the boy had complied, Matt turned to her. "Now, tell me what you're talking about."

"Well..." she said, biting her lip and staring at her lap.

"Does this have anything to do with the quarrel you had with my brother?" Barbara asked. "Or Noah?"

Ivy sighed. As hard as this was, she still must face it.

"Yes, Barbara, it does. Both. Or rather, one led to another. It's a bit confusing...."

Sitting on the edge of her chair, Ivy explained everything that had gone on earlier in the day. "I need to know the truth. Oh—" she glanced toward Barbara with sympathy "—not about Gerry. Sorry, Barb, but I'll have to make a full disclosure to the Dwelling board and committee, you realize that."

"Never mind, Ivy, I'll do it myself. I think the information is long overdue. I've long suspected that Gerry was up to something, but I could never figure it out. Whenever I questioned him about it, he either gave me some confusing answer, or assured me that I needn't worry."

Ivy nodded, then turned to Matt. "Can you tell me the truth about Noah?"

"What do you want me to say, Ivy? I've never known anything dishonest about Noah or his dealings. I know he broke with Gerry over something that concerned money. He's paid heavy money into a charity on whose board he and Gerry used to sit."

"I can tell you something about that, Ivy." Barbara interjected. "As you probably have guessed, Noah and Gerry were good friends in the past. Noah moved here because of Gerry, in fact. And they had lots of business plans they'd talked about. Noah loved the idea of service, of making charitable work a part of his life. But Gerry has a lot of pizzazz, you know? And Noah left it to him to set up the parameters of the charities and nonprofit organizations they had on their list.

"They were in the middle of the first really big one when the blowup came. Noah felt so guilty over unknowingly taking money he felt should have gone to the organization, he swore to pay it all back."

"Those were the receipts I saw," Ivy murmured. Then she looked up to explain, "I accidently saw a bundle of business receipts for The Old Garden Gate when he was staying with Aunt A and me. Now I realize it was mixed with personal ones."

She'd seen the receipt for her ring, too. Now she knew. Noah had given it to her.

Ivy turned back to Matt. "What else do you know?"

"Well, I know Noah's the kindest, most generous man I've ever met. I began working for him when he first bought the tree farm and we worked together all that first year until my accident."

Matt shifted uncomfortably in his chair. "I can tell you I wouldn't be alive today without Noah's help. This house is his, did you know that? He pays the mortgage and lets me and Chad live here rent free."

Astounded, Ivy remained silent. Barbara sat quietly as well. Finally, Barbara said, "I think Noah used money inherited from his grandparents to get the farm, Ivy. It wasn't ill-gotten, if that's what you've been afraid of. If my brother led you to think differently, then he lied."

Little by little, the heaviness in her heart drained away. Her eyes began to swim, only this time the tears were ones of relief. Noah had repaid money he thought was his moral obligation to pay; he wasn't a thief by anyone's definition.

He gave a friend shelter at his own cost, taking a less desirable place for himself.

A lightness lifted her spirits. He genuinely liked driving the seniors on their outings. He was right there to offer tender care of Shirley when she needed a strong shoulder on which to lean. He'd never turn his back on a woman he loved.

And he and Aunt Arletta... A smile edged her lips as she thought of the way he and Aunt Arletta got along. Like two kids in a chocolate pot. Planning little surprises, like New Year's Eve parties to give people they knew a needed evening of fun.

She recalled the soft admonition from only hours before. *Look for Me and you will find the truth....*

God's spirit permeated Noah's actions, his very being. That was the truth she sought. It didn't matter anymore how much money Noah may still owe or even what it was for; she knew it to be an honest debt and he would pay it over time.

It didn't matter that he lived in a trailer. If he asked her to live there with him, she'd leap at the chance. If they were reduced to a tent or a cave, she'd go with a glad heart.

It no longer mattered if his house furnishings were rickety and inadequate; she'd happily make do with what they had as long as they were together.

If...

If he still wanted her after her doubt of him. If he could forgive her all her snobbery, her lack of...dare she call it...charity?

"I have to go," she said, leaping to her feet. "Thanks, Matt. And Barbara, I'm grateful."

Pulling out of Matt's drive, Ivy glanced at her watch. She had to hurry or she'd never make the end of the church service. Praise was the very thing she needed at the moment. Praise for the Lord's wisdom and guidance. Praise that she'd been wrong in her judgment one more time, only this time it was to her benefit.

Three blocks from the church, a police car pulled her over. Ivy's heart sank. She'd broken the speed limit.

"Officer, I am sorry." Digging into her purse, she found her licence. "I'm not usually so—"

"Oh, it's you," said the beefy uniformed officer. "Old lady Arletta's kid."

"Niece," Ivy said, biting her lip. It would be someone who knew her aunt. Now she'd never get to church before the service let out. If she couldn't catch up to Noah now, he might drop Aunt A off and leave again before she'd had a chance to tell him how much she loved him.

"Yeah, I remember. You and that guy get home all right that night of the big December snow?"

"Yes, we did, eventually." She looked at him closer. His face did look familiar. A faint hope took shape in her thoughts. "Look, sir, I know I was speeding and I'll gladly pay my fine, but, you see, I'm trying to reach church before the service ends. That guy you saw me with that night? Well, his name is Noah, and I have to tell him—"

The officer held up his hand, palm out. "Hold it. Hold it right there. I guess you're Miz Arletta's niece, all right. If you don't mind, I don't want to hear anymore. I'll, um, let you go this time if you promise to slow down."

"Oh, I will. I promise."

Five minutes later, Ivy crept down the church aisle as quietly as possible. A trio was just ending a song and the congregation was instructed to rise. A song flashed on the overhead screens.

Biting her lip, she glanced down the row where Noah stood tall next to her aunt. He hadn't seen her and didn't look her way. His face lifted as he sang; above the other voices she heard her aunt's soar.

Unusual shyness clamped her own voice; as much as she wanted to, she couldn't find it. Courage, she told herself. She slipped into the pew past Shirley to stand between her aunt and Noah. Then tentatively, she raised her gaze.

Brown eyes, loving and compassionate stared into hers. A faint question lay in their depths. Opening her mouth, she tried to whisper, to say something. Anything. But the words wouldn't come. She could only drink in the yearning she saw there with the sense of being where she belonged, of having the rich feeling of being home.

Giving up, she let her hand drop and folded her fingers into his. His eyes shining, he enclosed hers in a firm clasp. As though they were welded together forever.

Explanations could wait. They had a lifetime to make them.

Beside her, Ivy heard her aunt's low tone, golden with assurance. "'By wisdom a house is built, and through understanding it is established; through knowledge its rooms are filled with rare and beautiful treasures.'"

"Yes..." she murmured into his gaze, finding her voice at last. "You are my rare treasure."

Epilogue

Standing in the large backyard next to her husband, Ivy gazed hopefully toward the rear of a gray thirty-year-old house of modest size that they had just toured for the third time. Their real estate agent, Mr. Barry, could be seen talking to the seller's agent through the opened French patio doors.

Nearby, autumn foliage lent beauty to a neighborhood of like homes. Kids' shouts and bouncing balls filled the Saturday air. Next door, Kelly and Scott pretended to discuss the merits of keeping the hedge fencing that divided the two lots, but they weren't successful at hiding where their real attention lay.

Ivy smiled tentatively at Noah. Were they really gaining a house of their very own? Was it too much to ask Heaven for when she was so sky-high happy already?

Noah sensed her nervous anticipation, because he slid his hand down to enclose hers. His strong fingers felt warm and gentle.

A moment later, Mr. Barry approached them. He

wore a smile. A very broad smile. "Mr. and Mrs. Thornton, you own a house," he said. "They've accepted your offer."

"Thank you, Lord," Ivy said aloud as she kissed her husband. She danced jubilantly over to Kelly and Scott. "We've got it! Imagine, Kelly. Right next door to you."

"Now I know this overgrown hedge has to go," Scott said with a laugh. "Or you two will kill it with traffic. But you still have a ways to catch up to us." He emphasized his point by patting his wife's extended abdomen. "Then we can fill up the space with playthings and little grass crawlers."

"Yep, and that's certainly in the immediate plans," Noah responded, laughing at Ivy's blush, "now that we're all caught up financially. But we still need to put the addition onto the house for Aunt A."

"By the way, where in she today?" Kelly asked. "I thought she'd be smack in the middle of all the negotiations."

"Well..." Ivy murmured sheepishly. "Did you know the Smiths, two doors down, are holding a Neighborhood Watch organizational meeting today?"

"You didn't," Kelly accused.

"Actually, it was Noah's suggestion," Ivy replied.

"Hey, Aunt A is very good at organization," Noah insisted. "She'll bug everyone into doing their job not only right, but timely. We can all count on her to spy out anything suspicious going on in the neighborhood while people are away during the day, too. And the neighbors are very impressed she already knows several city policemen."

"I'll bet," Kelly said, chuckling. "But really, I am rather glad she'll be right next door these next few months. With most women working, maternity leave feels a little lonely. You're lucky to have her, Ivy."

"We sure are," Noah chimed. "She's a treasure for sure. And I got lucky and blessed the day we ran into each other in that garden—she introduced me to Ivy. She got us together. She's been in my corner ever since. But the wonderful thing I thank the Lord for every day is..." He paused and gazed at Ivy with so much love in his eyes that it made her blush.

"...the real blessing is...Ivy is just like her."

* * * * *

Dear Reader,

Women in today's world face more pressures than ever to balance both family life and careers. We see expectations to do it well in everyone's eyes. In that race toward success, we sometimes get our wants mixed up with our needs, as Ivy did. Also, some of us find ourselves in the sandwich position between the generations, with more pulls on our time, attention and emotion than is easily handled. It is my belief that God can and does help with these situations; He's still vitally interested in helping men and women cope with their lives. He even brings a sense of humor to our attention when we need it, as Aunt Arletta shows. Most of all, He reminds us that above everything, love is the key to opening the answer door.

I hope you've enjoyed Ivy's discovery of life's real treasures. I also found Noah very attractive and had a wonderful time with the two of them and their developing love story. And I sincerely hope you had as much fun with Aunt Arletta as I did; she's a lot like me. Now I pray you find great fun in your own treasures, and much laughter along the way in your faith journey.

If you'd like to write me, you can do so at:
Ruth Scofield, P.O. Box 1221, Blue Springs,
Missouri 64013.

Ruth Scofield

Love Inspired®

Title Available in July 1999...

THE COWBOY'S BRIDE

by

Carolyne Aarsen

Joe Brewer grew up poor but rich in faith in the small prairie town of Wakely. Banker Rebecca Stevenson's faith had been dwindling ever since a devastating accident changed her life. Can two such different people ever find a common ground upon which to build a relationship?

Find out in the Love Inspired® title THE COWBOY'S BRIDE in July 1999

Available at your favorite retail outlet.

ILITCB

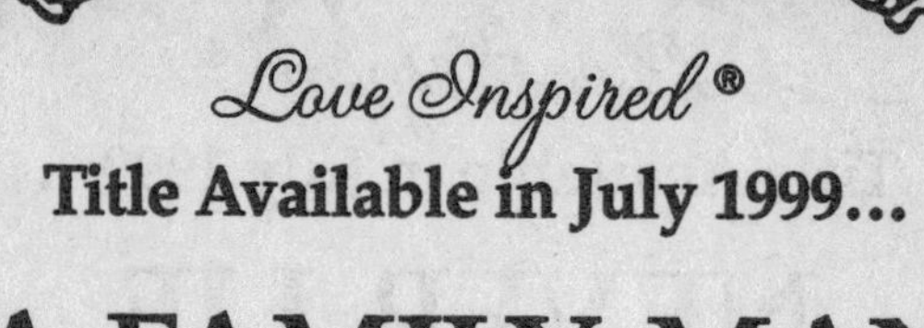

Title Available in July 1999...

A FAMILY MAN

by

Marcy Froemke

When Margaret Gould returns to Chattanooga with her young son, she is reunited with her old boyfriend, Adam Morgan. The attraction between them is still there, but they must deal with the emotional baggage from their past before they can attempt to bring their romance back to life.

Watch for the Love Inspired® title
A FAMILY MAN
in July 1999

Available at your favorite retail outlet.

ILIAFM

Love Inspired®
Title Available in July 1999...
NEVER LIE
TO AN
ANGEL
by
Kate Welsh
Greg Peterson goes undercover to investigate an inner-city mission and finds love unexpectedly with Angelica DeVoe, the beautiful mission founder and director. Can their love survive when Greg reveals his true identity?
Don't miss
NEVER LIE TO AN ANGEL
in July 1999 from
Love Inspired®
Available at your favorite retail outlet.